"Just this once, Vaughn, will you kiss me?"

"A kiss?" He needed to be sure, as much as it pained him to ask, to risk her denying the words.

"It's been a long, long time since I've had a real kiss that wasn't about drowning sorrow and forgetting." She spoke with an earnest sincerity that slid right past his defenses. "I just think it would be nice to have a taste of...what might have been."

He could have resisted his own impulse to taste her. He damned well couldn't deny her request, which made him want to move mountains to make her happy. To please her.

Except she wasn't his. And she never could be.

* * *

Expecting a Scandal is part of the Texas Cattleman's Club: The Impostor series— Will the scandal of the century lead to love for these rich ranchers?

Dear Reader,

Writing my first story for the well-loved Texas Cattleman's Club series was a huge thrill for me! I worked hard to ensure my story lived up to the other wonderful books I've read in this series over the years, and I loved walking the streets of Royal, creating more characters to add to a town I already knew and loved.

I was fortunate to have some real-life insights into the life of a trauma surgeon since my sister (and real-life personal heroine) works as a pediatric intensive care nurse. When I told her I was researching Vaughn, she invited me out to dinner with lots of her nursing friends, and I spent a wonderful evening hearing tales from the trenches.

Researching my artist heroine, Abigail, proved just as much fun. I knew she was a sculptor, but what kind? That question led me on a day-long journey viewing interactive sculptures for children online. It made me want to close up the laptop and become an artist! Not for long, though, since my skill with words is far better than my artistic prowess, which is probably best suited to coloring books.

I hope you enjoy your time in Royal, Texas, as much as I have.

Happy reading!

Joanne Rock

JOANNE ROCK

—

EXPECTING A SCANDAL

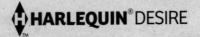
HARLEQUIN® DESIRE

Special thanks and acknowledgment are given to Joanne Rock for her contribution to the Texas Cattleman's Club: The Impostor miniseries.

ISBN-13: 978-1-335-97142-5

Recycling programs for this product may not exist in your area.

Expecting a Scandal

Printed in U.S.A.

www.Harlequin.com

Four-time RITA® Award nominee **Joanne Rock** has penned over seventy stories for Harlequin. An optimist by nature and a perpetual seeker of silver linings, Joanne finds romance fits her life outlook perfectly— love is worth fighting for. A former Golden Heart® Award recipient, she has won numerous awards for her stories. Learn more about Joanne's imaginative Muse by visiting her website, joannerock.com, or following @joannerock6 on Twitter.

Books by Joanne Rock

Harlequin Desire

Bayou Billionaires

His Secretary's Surprise Fiancé
Secret Baby Scandal

The McNeill Magnates

The Magnate's Mail-Order Bride
The Magnate's Marriage Merger
His Accidental Heir
Little Secrets: His Pregnant Secretary
Claiming His Secret Heir
For the Sake of His Heir

Texas Cattleman's Club: The Impostor

Expecting a Scandal

Visit her Author Profile page at Harlequin.com, or joannerock.com, for more titles.

To the A Team nurses at All Children's Hospital in St. Petersburg for your commitment and caring, for making a difference every day and for taking time out to share your stories with me.

One

Adjusting her glasses on her nose, Abigail Stewart hoped the funky red-and-black zebra frames distracted from the sheer desperation that must surely be visible in her eyes.

She didn't want the assembled Royal Memorial Hospital committee to see how badly she needed the commission for the sculpture she'd just proposed for the children's ward. Or how much it upset her to be back inside a hospital for the first time since her sister's death. Standing at the head of the hospital's boardroom after her presentation, she smoothed the hem of a fitted skirt that pinched her pregnant hips under the gauzy red top she'd chosen to hide her baby bump. At five months along, she wouldn't be fooling anyone for much longer. But considering the scandal attached to her baby's conception with a lying jerk posing as Will Sanders, the powerful head of Spark Energy Solutions, Abigail wasn't in a hurry to field questions about it. She was only just beginning to wrap her head around being a single mom in the wake of a hellish year that had cost her a beloved younger sibling.

A year that promised to go downhill even more, since Abigail would definitely not make the next mortgage payment on her house if she didn't nab this commission. She'd taken too much time off in the past year to help her mother cope with losing Alannah in a kayaking accident, depleting her emergency savings.

"Does anyone have questions about the art installation I'm proposing?" Abigail forced a smile despite the nervous churn in her belly.

At least, she hoped that rumble was nerves and not belated morning sickness. For the last two months, *morning* had been a relative term.

"I have a question." The deep, masculine voice at the back of the spacious room caught her off guard.

She'd thought all of the committee members were seated at the large table with a good view of the projection screen. Yet, at second glance, she saw an absurdly handsome man in green scrubs sprawled in a chair by the door in the back. From the leather shoes he sported to the expensive-looking haircut, he had an air of wealth about him that the scrubs and slightly scruffy facial hair couldn't hide. Even the phone resting on the table beside him cost more than her monthly house payment. She'd been so focused on getting her video up and running that she had somehow missed his arrival.

With a crop of thick brown hair and deep green eyes, he had a body that a professional athlete would envy—his broad chest and strong arms were supremely appealing. And for a woman five months pregnant and battling morning sickness along with a case of nerves to notice—that was saying something.

The hospital administrator who had invited Abigail to present to the committee gestured the newcomer toward a vacant chair at that table, where one presentation packet lay untouched. "Thank you for coming, Dr. Chambers, please join us."

"Sorry I'm late. My last surgery ran long." He rose and tugged the plush rolling chair out from the gleaming maple table, joining eleven other members of the committee in judging her. "And, Ms. Stewart, I'm sure you're very talented, and your gallery of works is certainly impressive, but I'm afraid I don't see the point of a statue in the children's ward when we are in need of more staffing and more on-site equipment."

Her stomach dropped.

The rumbling of reaction around the table gave Abigail a welcome moment to collect her thoughts before responding. She'd thought the commission was a foregone conclusion, whether she won it or another artist did, so she wasn't entirely prepared for the question. But since no one else jumped in to answer, she needed to field it fast.

"I believe the funds for artwork are designated strictly for that purpose by the benefactor who provided the grant." She glanced at the hospital administrator in charge of the committee, Belinda McDowell, who served as Royal Memorial's development officer. When the older woman didn't correct her, Abigail plowed ahead. "So the funding isn't something that can be reallocated."

Dr. Chambers stared back at her, his jaw flexing with thinly veiled impatience. Did he think art was so inferior to his field? Her spine steeled with some impatience of her own.

"Assuming that's the case…" He glanced at Mrs. McDowell for confirmation. At a nod of the woman's steel-gray bob, he continued, "Why a statue? Will children really appreciate art at that level, or would we be better served giving them something more age-appropriate that stands a chance of engaging them?"

Resisting the temptation to open his presentation packet for him and point out where she'd addressed this very question, she told herself she was being touchy because she needed this job so much. The visibility, the credibility and the portfolio development were all critical, even without the benefit of the income. Making a living as an artist in Royal hadn't been easy, even before Alannah's death.

"The statue would be a starting point since the hospital board would like to unveil the first element of a larger installation in the children's ward at a party later this month." She lifted her own presentation packet and flipped it open to the page with her proposed timeline. "There are some further details on page six."

Okay. So she hadn't been able to resist temptation.

But Dr. Green Eyes was single-handedly turning her presentation on its ear. He scrubbed a hand over his short beard, looking skeptical.

"Are there any other questions?" she blurted too quickly, realizing belatedly she was probably being rude.

Damn. It. How had she let him rattle her? Probably had something to do with the hospital bringing up bad memories. Or her too-tight skirt and her surprising reaction to the doctor. She'd thought, after the colossal mistake she'd made in sleeping with her former boss at her temp job, she'd effectively sworn off men for a while.

It bothered her to feel very feminine flutters of response to superficial things like an attractive face. Or a beautifully made male form.

That rich male voice rolled through the boardroom again. "Can good art be crafted in such a short time?" Dr. Chambers asked, now scanning through the pages of her presentation folder. "Do you really think you can meet that kind of deadline?"

Could she? It wouldn't be easy, of course. She had ten days. And she sure didn't appreciate the implication that "good" art was measured by how long it took to create it. Brilliant works had been crafted over the course of years, and others in the span of hours.

"Of course," she returned coolly. "Although, obviously, the sooner the committee reaches a decision, the easier it will be for the chosen artist to meet the deadline."

The committee leader, Belinda McDowell, rose. "And we hope to give you a response as soon as possible, Ms. Stewart. Thank you so much for coming in today." With a curt nod, she dismissed Abigail before turning her attention to the rest of the group. "I have one more artist I'd like you to meet if you can all remain for just ten more minutes."

Dismayed that she was already done with her portion of the meeting, Abigail hurried to gather her things before she headed toward the door. Had she blown the most important presentation of her career?

Passing Dr. Chambers on her way out, she felt her gaze drawn to him in spite of herself. Maybe because she wanted to give his chair a swift kick for finding fault in her presentation.

More likely, her artist's eye wanted to roam all over those intriguing angles of his face, the sculpted muscles of his body. At least, she hoped it was her inner artist that was having those ridiculous urges. Because if it was some kind of womanly desire for her surgeon heckler, who'd been about as charming as a Texas diamondback, then she had bigger worries than a depleted bank account and a baby on the way.

She needed a doctor all right. But only because she ought to have her head examined.

Vaughn Chambers flipped through the two artists' presentations side by side at a table in the hospital's doctor lounge later that afternoon. The lounge was busy at this hour during shift change, with colleagues darting in and out to grab coffee or a bite to eat. But Vaughn had positioned himself with his back to the room, earbuds in place, a coping mechanism he'd started using more often since his return from a military medical deployment with the United States Army Reserves.

Despite being the heir to an oil empire, Vaughn had never been willing to simply follow the path chosen for him. Instead of taking the easy route and accepting a CEO seat in the family company, he'd pursued a medical career. Inspired by his grandfather's military service, he'd been compelled to make a contribution of his own, signing on after he'd already secured his medical degree. He didn't regret those choices, but he was still paying for them.

He refused to let his service rob him of the career that meant everything to him, but coping with the aftereffects of his time as a brigade surgeon in Afghanistan had all but consumed him for months after he got home. Now, he understood the strategies for dealing with the post-traumatic stress. But since trauma was his surgical specialty, he could never fully insulate himself from the situations that triggered bad days.

Like today.

Vaughn stilled his restless knee under the table with effort, forcing a quietness in his body that he wasn't feeling, while a groggy resident struggled to make a fresh pot of coffee at the snack table beside him. Vaughn's patient this morning had been a stabbing victim, helicoptered in from a nearby ranch where a couple of cowboys had gotten into an argument over a card game. The surgery went well, though slowly, considering all the areas that needed repairing. But then, Vaughn had always been a rock during surgery, shutting down everything else in order to focus on the work he'd dedicated his whole life to perform.

The aftermath was what killed him, when he could no longer compartmentalize by focusing solely on the surgery at hand. And today, of all days, he'd had to sit in on a committee meeting about a new art installation right after he'd emerged from the operating room. He should have just blown it off. Except his colleague, Dr. Parker Reese, had asked him to attend as a personal favor. Or maybe Reese had been trying to do Vaughn a favor, nudging him back into the world outside a war zone, since Parker was one of the few guys who knew what Vaughn was going through. Either way, he'd promised. So Vaughn had dragged himself into that boardroom, adrenaline level crashing, knowing he wasn't at his best.

Now, drumming his fingers on the lounge table as he stared at the two artists' presentation packets, his eye landed on a photo of Abigail Stewart. Her long, espresso-colored curls fell over her shoulder as she smiled in a candid shot that captured a far more lighthearted woman than he'd met today. Sunlight behind her—like dawn breaking—made her glow. Her dark eyes glanced at something just off to the side of the camera, and whatever it was made her laugh. The photo wasn't your standard head shot, but made sense for an artist. She practically vibrated with warmth and vitality in the image.

Something he'd stomped during their brief meeting. He'd known, even as he questioned her after her presentation, that he'd been abrupt. Tactless. But that was because he'd been battling to keep himself together. Normally when he got out of a more difficult surgery, he either escaped under the headphones, or he booked it back home to decompress with his service dog, Ruby. Today, neither option had been available. So he'd launched his reservations about the art project at Ms. Stewart with zero filter.

A clap on Vaughn's back startled him. He whipped around too fast, too fierce. He could see it in Belinda McDowell's wide-eyed expression, her tiny step back.

"I—" The seasoned hospital administrator was an endlessly competent woman, a tireless advocate for Royal Memorial and a consummate professional.

And Vaughn had just spooked her because he was having a bad day.

Damn it.

"Sorry about that." Yanking off his earbuds, he turned on what little charm he could scavenge, smiling broadly. "I must have been falling asleep." He gave a rueful head shake. "Good thing my residency days are behind me. I'd never cut it."

The administrator thrust an envelope toward him. "No apology necessary. I'm very grateful to you for agreeing to pay a visit to Ms. Stewart so she can begin work on the art installation."

After the presentations, the committee had voted unanimously to select Abigail Stewart to begin work on the statue for the children's ward as phase one of a larger art installment. And because Vaughn had regretted the way he'd approached her, he had volunteered to deliver the news personally.

Ah, hell. Who was he kidding?

He couldn't deny that he had volunteered because she fascinated him. In spite of the rocky start to their meeting. In spite of the day he was having that reminded him he might never be normal again. Something about Abigail Stewart called to him.

"It's no problem to drop by her studio. I have to pass through downtown on my way home anyway." Accepting the envelope from Mrs. McDowell, he glanced down at Abigail's name typed on the front. "What's this?"

"Half of her commission payment, which were the terms we discussed in the meeting," she said crisply, nodding to a couple of the older cardiologists who'd been on staff at Royal Memorial for decades. "Please remind her she is welcome to work on site as often as she requires. There is a security badge and parking pass for her in there, as well."

So he'd be seeing more of Abigail. Possibly a lot more. With only ten days until the Royal Memorial summer gala, the artist would have her work cut out for her. Vaughn would have a ready-made excuse to see her again—often—at the hospital. If he chose. He wasn't sure how he felt about spending more time with a woman who cut through his usual defenses on the job, and elicited an elemental response in him in spite of how much he normally shut down at work.

"Of course." He laid the envelope on the table near his phone. "I know we want to give her as much time as possible, so I'll head over there as soon as I check on one last patient."

He wanted to see his stabbing victim before he left

the hospital. There were too many emotions dog piling on this day, making him antsy and ready to leave.

"Thank you." Mrs. McDowell checked her vibrating phone before silencing it. "And do be sure to get some rest, Dr. Chambers. You're an important part of our staff."

She turned efficiently on her gray heel and strode off, leaving Vaughn to stack up his papers. He paused before he could slide the presentation packets into the file folder, Abigail's photo catching his eye once more.

The noise of the lounge—residents laughing, an older doc dictating his notes in a monotone—all faded as Vaughn focused on the woman's image. He leaned closer to her photo, studying the lines of her face. She was undeniably attractive. Sultry, even, with those dark eyes, endless curls and kissable lips. But there was more to it than that. Vaughn had been approached by plenty of women since he'd returned from Afghanistan. And not one of them had tempted him out of his self-imposed isolation.

He'd almost been worried about the lack of interest, except that he knew PTSD was a long haul in the recovery process and he'd made definite progress since he'd started working with his golden retriever. Ruby had helped him sleep more soundly, waking him before his nightmares got out of control, preventing people from crowding him when he went out. Hell, Ruby had given him a reason to get out of the house in the first place, and that had been good for him. He'd figured the rest would follow in time.

Today, despite the adrenaline letdown and the cold sweat on his back throughout that interminable meeting, Vaughn had felt a definite spark of interest as he'd watched Abigail Stewart in that boardroom.

A welcome sign of some normalcy.

No matter that he wasn't in any shape for a relationship, he planned to at least see what happened when he saw her again.

Two

Circling her studio like a restless cat, Abigail cleaned and organized, too keyed up to work after the tense meeting at Royal Memorial. She'd tried drawing to decompress when she returned to her home-based art studio, but she couldn't concentrate. She'd ended up scrapping the little sketch she'd started once she realized her charcoal was bringing Dr. Chambers's likeness to life on the paper.

Now, she straightened her chisels in the storage block of wood, arranging them the way she liked— short-handled tools in front, longer blades in the back. The exercise wasn't strictly necessary, but she felt like she ordered her mind when she organized her world. And she needed that right now. Normally, sketching or painting helped her to wind down and readied her thoughts for the bigger work of her studio—wood carving. But today her inner muse was still sighing over the meeting with the surly surgeon, and she could not afford to ruin the beautiful piece of elm she was working on by accidentally carving the doctor's shoulders into it.

Not that the women of Royal, Texas, wouldn't line up to admire those spectacular muscles. Maybe it could be Abigail's breakthrough piece. But since her normal milieu tended toward fantasy creatures and more abstract pieces, she wasn't sure a set of broad male shoulders belonged in her catalog. They definitely didn't belong in her romantic musings when she was four months away from giving birth and eager to make peace with her sister's death. Somehow, she had to find a way to honor Alannah's life and move forward. She'd hoped maybe the Royal Memorial project would help her with that, but if Dr. Chambers had his way, she was already out of the running.

She turned up the folk music she'd been favoring for her creative time lately, hoping to quiet the demons while she got her studio in order, but the buzz of her doorbell cut right through the drums.

Setting aside a small carving knife, Abigail rose from her workbench and edged around wood blocks and logs in various stages of drying around the sunny backroom that she used for making her art. She'd knocked down a wall and moved the kitchen in her house to accommodate the needs of her work. When she tugged open the side door that had the buzzer, she fully expected to see a delivery of some sort. A new awl, maybe, or the used palm sander she'd bought on eBay.

Instead of a cardboard package, though, she found the man who'd preoccupied her thoughts all afternoon.

"Dr. Chambers." She felt the hum of awareness immediately. It didn't matter that he wore a ridiculously expensive watch and drove the low-slung, European-made sports car sitting in the driveway behind him, even though she'd told herself she was done with rich playboys, like the father of her child.

The vivid green of the hot doc's eyes watched her with interest. And, she guessed, radiated less animosity than he'd demonstrated back at the hospital. He'd left behind the scrubs she'd seen him in earlier. Now, he wore dark dress pants and a fitted blue button-down shirt open at the collar, a nod to the heat of a Texas July, perhaps.

The close-trimmed facial hair hid some of his face, and she guessed he would be even more overtly attractive when clean-shaven. Maybe that's why he wore the beard. Sometimes that level of compelling good looks could be a distraction from the substance beneath. Abigail would bet the women he worked with noticed him either way.

"It's Vaughn." He thrust out a hand, the silver Breitling watch glinting in the late-afternoon sun. "And I hope we didn't get off on the wrong foot earlier."

The words caught her off guard, even as she took his hand briefly. The contact hummed up her arm and tickled its way along her shoulder.

"Abigail," she said automatically, even though he clearly knew who she was. She hesitated, feeling awkward as she pulled her hand back. "And I'm surprised to see you. Unless—"

A surge of hopefulness made her tense. He wouldn't have come all the way out to her studio to deliver bad news, would he?

"You won the job." He relayed the information with a curt nod, as if he was reading the results of a CAT scan to a patient. The words were so spare and utilitarian, but the impact was tremendous. "I thought I'd deliver the news personally—"

Abigail didn't hear the rest of what he said, a wave of relief rolling over her so fast she nearly stumbled backward from it. She clasped her hands together and squeezed the good news tight as a giddy yelp of laughter leaped out.

"Thank you!" She did a little dance in place, sandals slapping out a joyous rhythm. "You have no idea what this means to me."

She would keep her house and the studio she loved. The commission was enough to smooth the way for her baby's first year without having to worry about money every month. And, perhaps best of all, she would have a beautiful piece to dedicate to her sister's memory. The tree sculpture would be for Alannah. A tree of life and hope.

On her doorstep, Vaughn stared at her feet, tracking the happy hop like he'd never seen anything like it before. "I thought it was the least I could do given my demeanor earlier—"

She waved away the concern. None of it mattered now.

"Would you like to come in?" She saw the folder beneath his arm. Guessed there might be a check inside that paperwork. How surprising that the ornery surgeon had ended up being the bearer of the best news she'd had in a long, long time.

The briefest of hesitations.

Maybe the rich doc wasn't used to spending his time in an artsy bungalow downtown. With her folk music still blaring inside and her watercolors taped in all the windows, her work space was definitely on the eclectic side. Or maybe he just didn't like art period. Today, she was too relieved to care.

"Sure." Another clipped nod as his expensive leather loafers climbed the wooden steps. "Thank you."

Abigail backed into her studio and turned down the volume on her music, eyeing him as he moved deeper into her space. She'd never had a man here in the two years since she'd relocated to Royal from

Austin. He had a way of filling up the room, even though her studio was airy and open. Vaughn's presence, while quiet, loomed large.

He took it all in, his gaze missing nothing as he followed her to the drawing table, where sketches lined the walls around it. She gestured to one of the chairs there, an armless seat she'd made herself of reclaimed wood.

"Have a seat. Can I get you some water? Sweet tea?" she asked as she headed into the kitchenette in the back corner of the studio. She would have gladly cracked open champagne if she wasn't five months pregnant. Not that she kept champagne on hand. But this new commission changed everything for her.

And even though she hadn't appreciated the doctor's contentious approach at the time, he was here, offering her the job that would keep her afloat—financially, creatively and maybe emotionally, too—at the most critical juncture of her life. She couldn't help but feel a softening in her attitude toward him.

"No. Thank you." He sat forward in the seat, all business. Withdrawing the folder from under his arm, he laid it on the table. "I brought the contract for you to sign, along with the initial payment."

He slid the papers out of the folder, carefully positioning them between her morning watercolor of a nuthatch on a tree branch, and an afternoon charcoal sketch of…him?

Oh. *No.* Horrified she hadn't tossed the paper in

the basket, she rushed back toward the table, hoping to move it before he noticed.

Had he already noticed?

"I. Um. That is—" She was by his side in a split second. Standing too close to him. Hovering over him. Sounding completely inarticulate.

"It's all very straightforward." He glanced up at her. Frowned. "Is anything wrong?"

She couldn't tell from his expression if he'd noticed the half-drawn image of himself. Leaning forward, she slid her scattered papers together in a hurry, knocking the check on the floor and bumping his thigh with her knee. Awareness of him made her senses swim.

She'd been careful to leave her artist's smock over her dress, so she didn't think he'd noticed her baby bump. Not many people in Royal knew about it, after all, and she guessed the flash of male interest she'd seen in his eyes would disappear once he learned of her impending motherhood. Was it so wrong to want to savor that attraction just a little longer?

"Ah. No." She shook her head, imagining she appeared about as innocent as a toddler with a hand in the cookie jar. "Just sorry about the mess."

Her cheeks burned. All of her was feeling rather warm, actually, and it wasn't just because of the awkward embarrassment. Her skin tingled beneath the hem of her skirt where she'd brushed up against his leg.

Backing up a step, she tried to act casual even

though her heart thudded too fast. He picked up the dropped check and returned it to the table.

"Your studio puts my office to shame." He studied her with green-gold eyes that tracked her every movement.

"I was straightening up when you arrived." She hurried over to her desk and shoved the papers in the top drawer before returning to the table. Taking the seat beside him, she tried to collect herself.

Hit the mental reset button.

To cool down and get her thoughts back on track, she turned the contract toward her and started reading.

The meeting with Abigail Stewart had gone from interesting to downright fascinating. The tension between them had shifted since the stressful morning meeting. He credited that to several things. Being further removed from the surgery that had threatened to give him flashbacks definitely helped him to relax more around her. Add to that the fact that Abigail was obviously thrilled she'd won the art gig, which put her in a happy frame of mind.

Best of all, he'd spied a half-finished sketch on her table of a man who bore a striking resemblance to him.

He would have written it off as a coincidence since he couldn't be certain, of course. But then he'd seen the way her eyes locked on the drawing and her rush to remove it. There'd been a flare of unmistakable embarrassment. Awareness. Hell, the electricity between them had spiked to a shocking degree in those moments when she'd been close to him. The attraction had been a revelation considering how resolutely—and easily—he'd ignored dating since his deployment.

The heat Abigail stirred wasn't going to be ignored.

Vaughn watched her read over the contract he'd brought, and lingered on her lovely features as she pursed her lips or tilted her head. For a moment, she traced a line of text with her finger, as if to slow her pace or concentrate. Dark curls pooled on the table beside the paper, the silky waves calling to his fingers to touch them. Test how they would feel against his skin.

She'd changed since he'd seen her at the hospital earlier. She wore an artist's smock over a loose summer dress. The pale green cotton printed with daisies peeked out of the smock at the hem, the kind of simple summer staple that was probably comfortable for working. Yet on Abigail, the outfit was as seductive as anything he'd ever seen a woman wear. The low-cut neckline visible above the square-necked apron revealed ample curves, and a gold medallion knocked against the table as she bent to read the papers he'd given her. Beneath the table, she crossed her long legs, and her sandaled foot brushed his calf for an instant as she moved, sending his imagination into overdrive…

And damn. He shouldn't allow his thoughts to roam in that direction until he knew more about her. What if she was married? Had a significant other? He didn't see another car in her driveway, and her ring finger was bare, but that didn't necessarily mean she was available.

Surely the drawing she'd made of him meant something, though.

"There." Abigail signed her name with a flourish. "All set." She pushed the paperwork toward him, straightening in her seat. "Would you like me to show you around the studio before you go?"

He couldn't decide if that was a genuine invitation or a politely worded hint for him to be on his way. He used to be better at reading social nuances. These days, just keeping his own emotions in check took focus. And although he was anxious to get home and decompress from this day, he had to admit he enjoyed this time with Abigail.

"I'd like that." Leaving her advance payment on the table along with the security badge and a few other documents, he slid the signed agreement into his folder. He'd give it to Belinda tomorrow to make copies. "It's not at all what I expected," he told her honestly, hoping to learn more about Abigail if he spent a little time with her.

"No?" She glanced at him over her shoulder as

she led him past a shelf full of paint cans and chemicals, her dark eyes challenging. "Did you envision me sitting around my garret with a bunch of wine-swilling pseudointellectuals while we debated the novels of Kafka?"

He laughed out loud, surprised at the sound. "Not quite. But I definitely didn't envision this many axes." He stopped near a bunch of sinister-looking hatchets and hand tools leaning against the wall alongside ladders in varying sizes.

She paused beside him, her embarrassment from earlier in their meeting long gone. She smiled with something like fondness as she looked over the tools of her trade. The whole place smelled like hickory and apple wood, a welcoming scent that reminded him of fall bonfires.

"Wood carving can be strenuous labor, but I love it." She straightened a few small blades on a shelf nearby. "I still work in other media, but I've been obsessed with wood for the last few years."

"The tree sculpture you proposed for the children's ward will be made from wood?" He hadn't read the specs of her work very carefully, and besides, she had a great deal of artistic license in the project, so it wasn't as though the hospital was dictating precise details for the project she crafted for the installation.

"Yes. I have a perfect length of bay laurel in mind.

It's been drying for years, and I've always known that I wanted it for a tree of some sort."

"Years? How long have you lived in Royal?" He didn't remember hearing about her work until after he returned from his deployment.

"It's been a little over two years." She stepped carefully around a short sculpture of a bird with an ox's head, moving deeper into the stacks of raw wood.

"Do you mean to tell me you that you brought some of this with you when you moved?" His gaze wandered over all the huge logs of varying sizes.

"I brought almost all of it since I had access to a lot of wood remnants where I lived in Austin. I haven't found a good source here yet." She moved aside some of the limbs with relative ease, making him realize that she had the larger hunks secured with ropes hanging from the rafters so they wouldn't fall. She spotted the bay laurel she had in mind for the hospital sculpture and showed him some of the features.

"You should come out to my place sometime," he said when she finished, even before he'd worked out if she was single or not. "That is, if you want to check out the trees."

"I don't take any fresh wood. Only fallen pieces." She stepped carefully from her place among the knotty branches and gnarled slabs in every shade and fiber. "Do you think you have any downed trees on your property?"

"That's not the sort of thing I typically look for when I go riding. But I've got over two hundred acres, so there's bound to be something if you'd like to take a look sometime."

"Really? You wouldn't mind?" She brightened, the same happy expression lighting her eyes that he'd seen when he first told her about the commission.

He liked seeing her smile. Hearing the way her pleasure warmed the tone of her voice. He found himself wanting to get a whole lot closer to her and all that warmth.

"I'm not on call at the hospital this weekend. Come by anytime." He withdrew his phone to message her with his contact information, dragging her phone number from his electronic copy of the commission contract. "I just sent you the address."

"Thank you. I find inspiration just being out in nature, so I'd be grateful for the chance to see any of the woodlands." She showed him a few more features of her studio, ending with the sunny corner where she liked to paint.

His eye roamed over the paintings she'd taped up around the windows and walls. There were dozens.

"You paint, you draw, you carve," he observed. "You don't ever feel like you're spreading yourself too thin?"

As soon as he asked, he wondered if the question was too pointed. If he sounded critical again, the way he had in the meeting earlier. But the query was honest, and some of his bluntness was simply a part of his personality, long before the PTSD had hit him hard.

She shrugged, not seeming to take offense. "You repair everything from gallbladders to head trauma. I like to think I take that same kind of holistic approach to my expertise, too. It's all art, so it's all in my body of work."

"There are so many paintings." He ran a finger over one image of a woman's back. Or at least, he thought it looked the curve of a feminine spine. The colors were muted and the image was a close-up, so he couldn't be sure. Yet there was a sensuality to the flare of hips, and the subtle shape of an hourglass.

"I paint them quickly in the morning sometimes for a warm-up, just to get ideas flowing." She glanced up at some of the paintings above her head, a rainbow of color on the wall behind her.

"How about the drawings?" he asked, thinking back to the sketch she'd done of him. "What makes you decide to use charcoals instead of paints?"

Her hesitation made him think that she understood exactly what he sought to discover. *What had made her sketch him?*

She took her time answering, threading a finger under a loose curl to skim it away from her face. A prism hanging in a nearby window reflected flashes of light on her skin. "I'm inclined to draw when I'm unsettled. I often use the charcoals to vent emotions—nervousness, anger…grief."

Her voice hitched a bit, alerting him that he may have touched a nerve. Regretting that, he sought to reroute the conversation, not wanting to lose the tenuous connection he really wanted to strengthen with this woman. He couldn't remember the last time he'd had an in-depth talk with anyone outside of the workplace.

"It's good you've got a productive outlet for that." He wondered which of those negative emotions had driven her to sketch him. No doubt he'd upset her earlier in the day. "Too many surgeons I know detach so thoroughly that they become—" Jackasses? That seemed a harsh way to define some of his colleagues. "Dedicated loners."

"You wouldn't be able to perform your job without some ability to detach." Her hand alighted on his forearm in a gesture of comfort.

The contact was a social politeness. An expression of empathy.

But damn if it didn't light up all his circuits like the Fourth of July. For the space of two heartbeats, her touch remained. He looked down at the place where she'd touched him, her fingers already sliding away. He missed the warmth immediately. Craved more of her caresses.

"Detaching isn't a problem for me," he admitted,

unwilling to confess how deeply he wrestled with the fallout from that skill. "Sometimes that makes me far too abrupt, as you witnessed firsthand in today's committee meeting."

He watched her face, locking on her expression before he continued. "Were you venting negative emotions about that when you drew the picture of me?"

Perhaps she'd been expecting the question, or maybe she'd simply been more prepared to revisit the topic after her initial embarrassment about the sketch. She lifted a brow, her gaze wary, but she didn't flush with discomfort this time.

"You noticed that and didn't say anything?" She shook her head with a rueful laugh and leaned up against a built-in counter with cabinets below and shelves overhead. Paintbrushes in every size imaginable hung on a rack over the shelves. "I guess you are good at detaching. If I saw someone had made a picture of me, I would have been quick to ask a hundred questions about it."

His gaze traveled her body, where her position drew all the more attention to her curves.

"I was curious." He shoved his hands in his pockets to combat the urge to touch her. "I just didn't think it was the right moment to ask."

"Truthfully, yes, I felt frustrated about the meeting when I returned to the studio. I didn't have any preconceived idea of what I would draw. I just sat down to blurt out anything that came to mind." She met his eyes directly. Openly. "I was surprised when I saw you take shape on the paper."

He wanted to think he'd ended up there because they had a connection. An undeniable spark.

Because the longer he lingered in Abigail's sunny studio, the more he felt his normal boundaries crumbling. And while he wanted that—craved following up on the attraction simmering between them—he wasn't sure how he would handle anything beyond simple lust. The realization made him edgy.

She filled the silence that followed with a sudden question. "Would you like me to finish the drawing?"

His throat went dry. The question had gotten complicated in the space of a moment as he started to recognize that Abigail wasn't going to be the kind of woman who would be open to a purely physical relationship.

"I wouldn't want to keep you from your work." He couldn't think of a more eloquent retreat with Abigail moving toward him. Touching him again.

"Not at all." She took his hand briefly to lead him toward a chair near her painting spot, her touch fanning the flame inside him, making him think about so much more. "Have a seat and I'll finish up. You can see what it's like to watch an artist at work."

In the space of five minutes, Vaughn realized he'd somehow used up all his emotional reserves today. All of his ability to detach. Because that simple touch from Abigail sent all the wrong messages to his brain. He hadn't given himself the outlet of a sexual relationship since he'd returned from Afghanistan. And now, the consequences of that had him on sensory overload, when he'd already battled the aftermath of a hellish surgery this morning.

A perfect storm of too many emotions without enough time to process them. He should have taken the time to go home and pick up Ruby before he came here. Having his dog beside him would have helped.

But he was already sitting in the seat Abigail had shown him when she returned with a heavy pencil in one hand and her half-made sketch in the other. She set both on a low table nearby, then moved closer to him, her gaze all over him. Studying him.

Seeing inside him somehow.

"Do you mind if I position you just a little?" she asked, already setting aside the folder he'd been carrying.

He wasn't sure if he'd agreed or not. His forehead broke out in a sweat. Warning heat blasted up his back. He wanted her.

"Here." Abigail set her hands on his shoulders and gently shifted them toward her.

She stood close, her knee brushing his thigh as she moved him, her breasts at eye level. She smelled like cinnamon and oranges, a spicy, tangy fragrance that would be burned into his memory forever. Sunlight kissed her face as she lifted his chin with one palm, her eyes taking a critical assessment of his features while he battled lust and a whole knot of other things he couldn't come close to naming. Hunger for her gnawed at him. Hot. Persistent.

"I've got to go." He clamped a hand on her wrist. Too hard at first. But then, realizing his responses were all out of whack, he gentled his hand. Released her. "I'm sorry, Abigail. I forgot that I said I would—" He rose from the chair. Sidestepped her. "Upload my notes on a critical-care patient after some—" His brain worked to come up with something vaguely believable before he did something stupid. Like kiss her until they were both breathless. Senseless. "Technical difficulties at the hospital."

His voice rasped drily as he grappled for control.

"Of course." She nodded even though she appeared as perplexed as he felt. "I'm sure I'll see you at the hospital when I start work on site."

"Right." He didn't reiterate his offer for her to come by his ranch. He needed to get his head on straight first. "I'm sure you will."

Backing out of the door, he lifted a hand in a quick wave.

"Thank you for coming by. I couldn't be more excited about the project," she called after him.

But Vaughn didn't answer. He was down the steps and seated in his truck in no time, slamming the door behind him while he turned over the engine and blasted the air-conditioning on his overheated body.

He didn't know what the hell he'd been thinking, pursuing this sudden attraction he was clearly not ready to handle. Maybe some other day, when he wasn't already depleted from a surgery that had brought back too many memories. But for right now, he needed to put some distance between him and a woman who stirred a surplus of emotions. No matter how much he thought he had mastered detachment, Abigail Stewart made him realize he'd only succeeded in getting damn good at lying to himself.

Three

A few days later, Abigail wondered if it had been presumptuous of her to accept Vaughn's offer to search for pieces of fallen wood on his ranch outside of town. Driving out of downtown toward the address Vaughn had given her, she knew it was too late to turn back now. She did really want the chance to walk through the trees and find inspiration, along with some different kinds of boughs for the oversize statue she was creating for Royal Memorial. That much was true.

But there was no denying her interest in the lone wolf doctor who so fascinated her.

When she'd texted her request for when she'd like to come to his property, the response had been almost immediate, making her wonder if he was just that prompt. Or if he'd been thinking about her, too. She was intrigued to see him again even though she knew she needed to tell him about her pregnancy.

Now, turning down the road that passed the Ace in the Hole Ranch, where she used to work for the man she'd believed to be Will Sanders, she couldn't stop the flood of memories. The main house was massive, with a deep front porch and multiple rooflines, plus an open breezeway connecting to a guest cottage. The crisp, white-painted home and dark shutters were immaculate, the trimmed hedges in perfect alignment. In the years she'd lived in Royal, she'd never seen the rolling lawn allowed to grow a millimeter too long. At night, it was really something to behold, with the many windows lit from within, and landscape lighting that illuminated the prettiest features.

Working at the Ace in the Hole had been rewarding if only to step onto that gorgeous property every day for a few weeks last winter. Her actual duties had been straightforward enough—organizing files and transferring them to more secure storage for Will.

Or, more accurately, the man who'd been impersonating Will Sanders, his former friend, Richard Lowell. Not many people in Royal knew that Will Sanders had returned to town to crash his own funeral. The FBI was now involved in the quiet investigation since they hoped that they might lure Rich

Lowell back. Abigail knew about it because she'd received a letter from an attorney asking her to attend the funeral, since she was named as one of Will's heirs. She'd nearly fainted when Will walked into the service himself.

None of that changed the fact that she'd had a one-night stand with the man who'd impersonated Will.

And now, she needed to let Vaughn know about the pregnancy. She was trying to move beyond the anger and frustration surrounding the father of her baby. She still worried about what she would tell her child about his or her daddy down the road. That he was a felon? A sociopath? Guilty of more crimes than she even knew about?

Shuddering, she touched her belly protectively and felt an answering flutter. The shifting movements of this life inside never failed to amaze her since she'd started noticing it in the last few weeks. Amid so much grief this past year, those signs of vibrant renewal felt like the most precious gift in the world.

Pulling up to the gates of Vaughn's property, some of those happy feelings faded, however. The gates were huge. Imposing.

And the most definitely ensured privacy.

She knew many doctors earned a good living, but an electric gate with wrought-iron scrollwork outlining the house number suggested a whole different level of wealth. The arched entrance was a good ten feet tall on the sides, swooping up to fifteen at the peak of the arch. She pressed the call button on the keypad and Vaughn's voice answered as the gate mechanism whirred softly, pulling open to the paved road that must lead to his home.

"Glad you found the place, Abigail," he said, through the speaker on the security system. "You can park in front of the house and I'll meet you there."

"Okay. Thanks." Her voice sounded flat. Because she was intimidated? Or because she'd hoped to find Vaughn living somewhere more…accessible?

She knew it wasn't fair to hold it against him that he'd done well in life. But after seeing how Will Sanders's money had corrupted someone into impersonating him, she sure didn't take any pleasure from the wealthy trappings that other people might find appealing.

Rounding a bend surrounded by live oaks, Abigail had to admire the old growth buffering the home from the roadway. There were walnut and maple trees, ash and pecan.

And then, there *he* was.

Vaughn Chambers stood out in front of his ranch home built of sandstone, the dusky browns and tans of the rock walls blending with the hills and trees so seamlessly it looked like a part of the landscape. A planked porch wrapped around two sides, with the main roofline continuing down to the porch, a trick of building that provided plenty of shade to homes in the summertime. The darker roof and wooden porch columns set off the lighter stone. Three dormers graced the main roof, giving the house a modest-sized second floor and a huge footprint on the main level. A detached garage with huge, dark wood doors looked big enough to hold a monster truck. Or, more likely, multiple vehicles.

The house was lovely, and couldn't be more different from the manicured beauty of the Ace in the Hole. Vaughn's home had a rustic, natural appeal.

As for the man himself, her breath caught to see him again. The short beard and moustache appeared freshly trimmed today. His thick brown hair was darker and spiky from a recent shower. He wore a gray T-shirt with jeans and boots that looked like they'd seen real work. A golden retriever sat at his feet, its long fur brushed and gleaming in the July sunlight.

"What a beautiful dog!" She was grateful for the animal, a welcome topic of conversation to hide her nervousness.

"This is Ruby." He scratched his canine behind the ears, the affection in his voice obvious. "Ruby, meet Abigail."

"May I pet her?" She liked to ask first even though the dog appeared well-trained. Her sister had once startled a stray in her eagerness to pet it when they were kids, and she had a scar on her leg from the bite for the rest of her too-short life.

How daunting that a hundred and one things every day still made her think of Alannah. Her chest went tight with the familiar squeeze of sorrow.

"Sure. She's a social dog and she likes a good scratch on the haunches."

Bending closer to Ruby, Abigail stroked the silky fur. Her knee brushed up against the animal's collar as she patted one side of her back, the movement jingling the silver tags. One had her name engraved on it and, she guessed, Vaughn's contact information on the other side. It was the second tag that caught her eye for the red caduceus and the Service Dog—Full Access notation.

Vaughn had a service dog?

She knew it was rude to ask about it, a working-dog etiquette tip she'd picked up from her friend Natalie St. Cloud, who owned the Cimarron Rose B and B in Royal, where Abigail occasionally stopped for a meal. Natalie had an autistic son who had a service dog, another golden retriever, and the animal had made a world of difference in their lives.

Straightening from petting the dog, Abigail swallowed the questions pinwheeling through her brain. If Vaughn had noticed her reading his dog's tags, he didn't indicate it. He gave the dog the command to "free play," and Ruby sprinted over to a pair of weathered gray barns on the side of the house near a large, fenced pasture.

"I'm glad you're here." He turned toward her

again. "I regret the way I left in a hurry on Wednesday."

The hint of hunger in his green eyes made her feel things for him she shouldn't. She really needed to tell him about her pregnancy. End this heart-fluttering tension between them and focus on her work and her baby.

"It was kind of you to make the time to stop by personally in the first place." She took a deep breath, prepared to tell him the truth.

"Would you prefer the walking tour or a horseback version?" he asked and gestured toward the barn before she could get the words out.

She loved riding, but it had been years she'd been in a saddle and wasn't sure how she would fare. Five months pregnant might not be the best time to try refreshing her skills.

"Maybe I'd do best on foot today. My horseback-riding skills are decidedly rusty."

"I have a utility vehicle with a cart attached. If you see something you like while we're out, you can just let me know and I'll use the cart to pick it up for you later."

"That would be great." She had planned to simply use the day for inspiration in creating her own tree for the children's ward, but she appreciated the offer of bringing some pieces home with her. "Thank you."

They started down a worn path between the house and barns. Ruby remained close to Vaughn's side even though she wasn't on a leash. The golden retriever didn't dart off to examine butterflies or sniff interesting fence posts. Clearly, the dog was tightly bonded to Vaughn.

Abigail enjoyed walking with them both as they entered a wooded area on the southern side of the ranch. Part of her delight was being in nature, something she missed in her downtown bungalow. With the earthy scents of green and growing vegetation around them, she breathed deeper, her fingers trailing over tree trunks and brushing against mossy logs. But another aspect of her pleasure had to do with Vaughn's very male presence beside her. His warmth and strength. The simple consideration he showed for her when he lifted a low sapling branch out of her way or pointed out a rocky patch in the terrain.

"I didn't get to ask you something the other day." Vaughn held out his hand to her to help her across a rivulet.

She accepted his offer, squeezing his fingers for balance as she hopped over the water, his touch making her far too aware of him. "What's that? After our first meeting, I can't imagine you holding back on any question you wanted to pose," she teased lightly, telling herself not to let the brush of his fingers affect her.

"Are you seeing anyone?" He stopped beside her, his boot cracking a twig underfoot as he pivoted to look at her, his hand still holding hers.

Everything inside her stilled. Because with that question, he was making it clear that she hadn't misread the signals he'd sent. If she hadn't been expecting a baby, maybe this could lead to something more. Something special.

Her heart thudded so hard he probably felt it in his hand where her palm grazed his. Staring up into his eyes, she allowed herself a flash of if-only thoughts, where this moment would play out differently.

And then, she forced herself back to reality.

"No. I am definitely not." With a resolute shake of her head, she stepped back, disentangling their fingers with more than a little regret. "But my life is about to get very complicated, Vaughn, because I'm five months pregnant."

Too stunned to hide his shock, Vaughn dropped his gaze to her slim figure. She wore three-quarter-length yoga pants and a blue-and-white floral blouse that covered her midsection. Now that he thought back on it, all the times they'd met she'd been wearing loose tops or, like the other day, her artist's smock.

He'd just assumed she was single when he didn't see a ring and felt—*thought* he felt—the sparks between them. Damn. Damn. Damn. He knew it was rude to stare and, belatedly, he forced his eyes to meet hers.

"I had no idea." He shook his head, feeling like a first-rate idiot as a bird whistled and circled overhead. Ruby pressed against his leg, her head lightly nudging his knee. "I never would have guessed—"

"Well, I haven't made a habit of advertising it yet since I'm still trying to come to terms with what this pregnancy means for me." Abigail rubbed one hand over her other arm as if to ward off a chill, even though the day bordered on being hot. "Would you mind if we keep walking?"

"Sure." He nodded, his hand scratching Ruby's head automatically as they stalked deeper into the woodland portion of the ranch. "You're not…with the baby's father?"

She shook her head. "I'm not even sure he's alive." Her words were halting. Troubled. Then, as she slanted a look his way, something fierce lit her dark eyes. "But even if he is, he won't be a part of my child's life."

"He won't?" Vaughn knew she might not have a legal say in that since the father could sue for paternal rights. If Vaughn had a child, he would move heaven and earth to make sure he had a role in the baby's life.

Not that he would ever be a father after the way his world had changed forever. Besides, from the vehemence in her voice he suspected it wasn't the right moment to speculate about possible legal action involving her baby.

"Are you close with anyone in the Texas Cattleman's Club?" she asked, surprising him with the quick turn of conversation. Her tone was different now. Confiding. Confidential.

How sad that he felt like they were getting closer on the same day she pulled away. He still couldn't believe the woman he was so attracted to was carrying another man's child. He was too shocked at the news to figure out how he felt about that.

"I'm not active, but my father still is." His dad had asked him to stop by the club more than once since his return from Afghanistan.

His parents didn't really understand how hard he battled the PTSD, or that Vaughn didn't socialize more than strictly necessary. He pointed to a turn in the path through the woods, silently showing Abigail the way while she continued.

"Then you might know—and your father most likely already knows—that Rich Lowell was impersonating Will Sanders before the imposter faked Will's death."

Vaughn had heard rumblings, but not the full story. Will Sanders was a man who had it all—including a prestigious family with deep roots in Royal, and with the Texas Cattleman's Club. He owned one of the largest ranches in Royal in addition to being CEO of Spark Energy Solutions, an energy company with ties to oil, gas and solar.

Or at least, he was CEO. Before his supposed death eight weeks ago.

"I heard something about Will Sanders walking

into his own funeral this spring, but the story was too incredible to believe." Vaughn wondered how Abigail knew about it. The story hadn't been in the local news outlets even though Will Sanders was a high-profile member of the community.

And then, he understood. Abigail wasn't a member of the TCC. So if she knew about the FBI investigation that was allegedly probing into the impersonation and embezzlement schemes of a man posing as Will Sanders, it could only mean she'd been questioned. Or was close to one of the main parties under investigation.

She halted beside him, her brows lifted, as if fully expecting he would have put the pieces together.

He stroked the top of Ruby's head, taking comfort from her presence when he should probably be offering support to Abigail. "Is the man who pretended to be Will Sanders the father of your child?" he asked.

The hum of summer insects in the meadow nearby penetrated the woods, filling the air with a rising, buzzing sound, an ominous underscore to his question.

"Yes." The terse reply communicated a wealth of resentment.

Or was it something more complicated than that? He couldn't read her expression, but there was a plethora of emotions there.

"I'm so damn sorry." He spotted a place he'd wanted to show her, where a fallen log made a mossy seat beside a rushing brook. No doubt, this day wasn't going to be the kind of prelude to romance he'd hoped for, but he couldn't pretend he wasn't still drawn to the compelling woman beside him. He took her hand again, craving the feel of her in spite of everything. "Come sit for a minute."

"I don't regret this baby for a moment," she confided as she followed him toward the creek. "But I hate that I won't have a happy story to share with my child about his or her father. Quite the opposite, in fact."

Abigail's artist's gaze seemed to take in every detail as he led her under a low-hanging branch to show her the bend in the brook, perfect for dipping your toes on a hot day. The whole glade smelled like balsam and loamy earth.

"He deceived you along with the whole town." Vaughn couldn't imagine how devastated she must have been. But according to local gossips, Abigail hadn't been the only woman taken in by the fake Will Sanders's charm. The lowlife had been married to Megan Phillips and had an affair with a woman while abroad on business. "That's a lot to process in addition to the baby news."

He felt protective of Abigail, damn it. Was that why he kept hold of her hand, or steadied her waist when she stepped up onto the log? She deserved his care.

But as he sank to sit on the fallen tree beside her,

Vaughn knew he was lying to himself. He would take any excuse to touch her. Get closer to her.

"Our night together should have never happened in the first place." She wrapped her arms around herself, her feet dangling just above the brook's edge, while Ruby settled along the back of the log, faithfully watching Vaughn's back, the way she'd been trained. "I was doing temp work at the Ace in the Hole last winter. I didn't even know him that well. He told me he was separated from his wife, and I believed him."

Vaughn wasn't sure how to offer comfort. So he just listened. Waited. The rush of the water filled the silence while a soft breeze rustled through the hickory tree overhead. He couldn't deny a sense of relief that her relationship had been just one night and not a deep, emotional relationship. Yet at the same time, he knew it was irrational of him to feel that way since he barely knew her.

"I was working late that night because it was my younger sister's birthday." Her voice changed. Softened. "Alannah." She glanced over at him, blinking fast before she looked away again. "She would have been twenty-four. Only she died ten months before that, and I was really…struggling that day."

Whatever he'd thought she might say, it hadn't been anything remotely close to that. Understanding made his chest ache for her. He related to that kind of loss all too well.

His arm went around her shoulders. Behind him, he felt Ruby shift. Even his dog nudged Abigail's back, whimpering with the kind of empathetic emotion that animals keenly understood.

"Honey, I'm more sorry than I can say." He tipped his cheek to the top of her head. "She was taken from you far too soon."

He didn't even want to think about some bastard taking advantage of her grief. Because as much as Vaughn could admit he liked the feel of Abigail in his arms, he would never use her vulnerable state for leverage. That was just...so damn wrong.

"I knew right away that the night with Will— the imposter posing as Will—had been a mistake," she confessed, her voice muffled against his shirt before she straightened, then swiped quickly at her eyes. "I should have taken precautions the next day, but I was still so weighed down with grief. If anything, I felt worse." She shook her head. "It had been months since she drowned in a kayaking accident, so I thought I'd been coming to terms with it a little more. There was just something about having her birthday come and go that really set things back."

With an effort, he dropped his arm again, not wishing to overstep, the way that jackass boss of hers had.

"There are good days and bad days when you're grieving." He knew firsthand.

"Yeah." She nodded, startling a little as a frog

splashed into the water beside them. "And that was a bad few days. By the time I hauled myself out of it, I realized I missed the window when the morning-after pill was most effective." She tipped her face up to a patch of sunlight through the leaves. "I don't know. Sometimes I wonder if, subconsciously, I didn't mind the idea of having a baby. Nurturing another life when one so important had been taken from me."

"Whatever the reason, you've got a child to plan for." He had more questions about that, but he knew it wasn't his place to ask her those things.

It surprised him how very much he wanted to, though. How was she going to manage her work with an infant to care for? After the statue was completed in the children's ward, she still had a commitment to develop a bigger, interactive installation.

Her art involved chisels and saws. Power tools that make her studio off-limits for a child. She would have to hire help.

"I do." She nodded, a dark curl blowing against his shoulder as she shifted on the log beside him. "I'm going to focus all of my energy on preparing for this baby and creating a sculpture so beautiful and moving that my sister would be proud."

Her smile dazzled him, even more so since he could understand the bittersweet emotion that came with it. Ruby settled again behind them, her tail wagging slowly through the pine needles and dried leaves.

"That's a healthy way to express mourning." How often had his counselor told him he needed more constructive outlets in the early days of battling PTSD? He'd never found one. But maybe he could make another kind of positive step. He could share something of his journey that might help Abigail, even though that kind of thing was tough for him. "I know that, actually, because I've never been successful at finding my own. Healthy expressions of grief, that is."

The admission was awkward. But not as difficult as he'd imagined. Something about Abigail's presence relaxed him a fraction, taking some of the edge off his too-sharp emotions.

"I'm sorry, Vaughn." Her hand reached to cover his where it rested on his thigh. "Did you lose someone close to you, too?"

Too many.

He mulled over the best way to answer the question without ripping open his own hard-won control. He focused on a water bug swimming circles in a still patch of water off to the side of the brook.

"I took a yearlong deployment in Afghanistan with the army." The simple statement didn't come close to conveying what the experience meant. How deeply it had affected him. Changed him. "I can't claim the same blood ties to the guys lost during that time to the bond you had with your sister. But there's a definite brotherhood with men you spend your rec time with. Guys you share meals with."

Each piece of information hurt to share. As if speaking about that time made him relive it. Which was foolish, since he relived the worst of those times often enough in his mind.

Ruby must have sensed the tension because she left her spot on the ground behind him to sit by his knee, her face lifted to his. She was such a good dog. And he appreciated her helping him hold it together in front of Abigail.

"You don't need blood ties for that connection," Abigail assured him, her fingers threading neatly through his, filling in the empty places. Squeezing. "I'm sorry you lost brothers over there."

She tipped her dark head to his shoulder, and he breathed in the sweet, tangy sent of cinnamon and oranges.

The ache in his chest eased a fraction at the feel of her against him. He closed his eyes for a moment, while dueling songbirds called to one another overhead. He tried to steady himself because he wasn't the one who was supposed to be receiving comfort. He was supposed to be offering it.

"Ruby has been a big help," he admitted, wanting to put the rest of his brokenness on the table for the sake of honesty. Abigail had already battled the disappointment of one man's deception. He wouldn't make the same mistake of hiding the truth about himself. "She's a service dog, and she's trained to give me extra assistance for dealing with PTSD."

"I noticed her collar," Abigail confessed, "but I know it's rude to ask about it."

He smothered a chuckle.

Abigail lifted her head, confusion in her eyes. "What's funny about that?"

"Remember the way we met?" He wanted to touch her again. Stroke her hair. Pull her into his arms. But he knew he needed restraint after what she'd shared. "I was incredibly blunt and tactless. You owe me a rude question or two, Abigail, to even the score. You can ask me anything."

He could tell she wasn't sure how to interpret his shift in conversation. But he couldn't linger in those dark places. It was all he could do to share as much as he had with her today.

"I don't know if I have it in me to be rude. Too much of a good Southern girl." A small smile curved her lips.

She was so lovely. And in spite of everything she'd shared with him today, he still wanted her. He wanted to know how she tasted. What her lips would feel like on his. How the rest of her would fit against him. That was wrong on so many levels, especially given how hard he battled his own demons. He was in no shape to offer Abigail the kind of steady presence she needed in her life right now. But that didn't change the fact that she would be in his dreams tonight.

He wanted to stroke her cheek. Run a thumb along

her full lower lip to test the feel of it. To see her eyes widen with awareness.

"Be candid, then. You can ask me brusque, tactless questions anytime you like." He was joking. Trying to make her smile and doing his damnedest to evade any more conversation about his time as a brigade surgeon.

But something in Abigail's expression made him think she was taking the suggestion seriously.

"I do have something to ask you." She still held his hand, and at some point had moved closer to him, too. Her voice was a soft stroke of breath against his cheek. "Something frank and honest."

His heart thudded harder. He really should let go of her. Show her around the woods the way he'd promised. But she mesmerized him with her sultry dark eyes and her tender heart.

"Just this once, Vaughn, will you kiss me?"

Four

Too stunned to trust his ears, Vaughn waited a breath. A heartbeat. The brook at his feet rushed over rocks, babbling with far more clarity than his thoughts.

"A kiss?" He needed to be sure, as much as it pained him to ask, to risk her denying the words.

For an answer, she raised her free hand to his face, tracing his jaw through the thick scruff of beard that he'd worn since his homecoming. One more barrier between him and the rest of the world.

"It's been a long, long time since I've had a real kiss that wasn't about drowning sorrow and forgetting." She spoke with an earnest sincerity that slid right past his defenses. "I just think it would be nice to have a taste of…what might have been."

He could have resisted his own impulse to taste her, but he damn well couldn't deny her request that made him want to move mountains to make her happy. To please her.

So he lifted up a rusty prayer for restraint as he threaded a hand through her silky hair. He cupped the back of her neck. Drew her toward him. He moved slowly, giving her time to change her mind. She thought it had been a long time for her? He'd bet it had been even longer for him.

And every instant of those achingly lonely months without a woman's touch turned on him now, sending a roaring heat blazing over his skin. Sensual hunger reared up like a ravenous beast. Ruthlessly, he tamped it all down to brush his lips tenderly over hers. Once. Twice.

He breathed her in. Felt her breath catch. He skimmed a touch down the side of her neck while the whole world fell away around them. He wanted to bring her home and kiss her whole body this way. With the sweet reverence she deserved after the year she'd endured. His beautiful warrior.

Except she wasn't his. And she never could be.

Breaking the kiss, he closed his eyes for a moment longer, unwilling to look into hers and see all that he could never have with her. He was too broken to share a life with anyone, let alone a woman who had a child on the way. She deserved so much more than the scraps of himself that he just barely held together.

When he felt her shift away from him, he looked up to see her brush her fingers over her lips, a gesture that made him want to haul her right back into his arms again. He steeled himself against the impulse.

"Should we finish up the walk?" he asked, holding out a hand to help her to her feet. "I think I see a fallen pecan tree over there."

She nodded, already in motion. Perhaps she needed to get her thoughts together as much as he did. Ruby trotted between them, looking up at him with soulful eyes. Vaughn followed more slowly, knowing he'd never forget the feel of Abigail's lips on his.

Back in her studio that evening, Abigail lifted her safety goggles and stepped away from her project to stare up at the giant tree sculpture she was making for the children's ward. She set down her chisel on a workbench, knowing she was getting ahead of herself with some detail carving down low on the tree when she still had big cuts to make on the top half. She planned to graft branches of varying kinds of wood onto the trunk, creating a tree that was larger than life and represented all trees. In her own mind, she knew it was a multicultural tree. An accepting tree with many outstretched arms.

But she let people see in it what they chose.

She had a long way to go to complete the project and tonight she was still rattled after that kiss and the time spent with Vaughn, unsure what it all meant.

She was in dire need of an outlet, and her work usually provided the best kind of distraction.

Unfortunately, not today.

She had been lost in the moment when she'd asked for that kiss, affected by the warmth of the man and the beauty of the surroundings. Heartened by his understanding of a night she would always remember with some sadness mixed in with the miracle of conception. Telling Vaughn had been cathartic. She felt a connection to him that went far beyond their brief acquaintance. Maybe it was because he had experienced devastating loss, too.

Whatever it was that drew her to him, she'd had no right to ask for that kiss. Her hand dropped to the swell of her belly where her child rested. She was a mother now, and she needed to start thinking like one. She could no longer afford to follow a moment's impulse, no matter how compelling.

The remainder of that walk had been quiet. She'd pointed out a few fallen tree limbs that she wouldn't mind reclaiming, and he'd told her about improvements he'd made to the property over time. Conversation hadn't been tense, exactly, but was definitely more reserved with the memory of that kiss between them.

No doubt, she'd scared him away with her revelation about the baby. Which wasn't necessarily a bad thing given her pregnancy and her need to turn a new page in her life. She was ready to devote her heart and her time to her child.

So why was she still thinking about how Vaughn's fingers had felt, sifting through her hair, stroking lightly down her neck? How his mouth had molded to hers gently, like he was tasting something precious?

Yanking the safety goggles the rest of the way off her head, she got the band snagged in her hair. With a curse, she stepped over to the window so she could see better to untwine the tiny snarl.

Outside, a dark gray pickup truck was backing into her driveway. With the tailgate down, tree limbs spilled from the cargo bed, a red ribbon tied around the longest end, the whole load strapped down and neatly clamped. A dog's nose poked out of the partially open window, as if to catch the scent of new surroundings.

Vaughn and Ruby had arrived.

A ridiculous jolt of excitement chased through Abigail even though she had just finished telling herself to draw boundaries with the sexy doctor. She carefully freed the knot and the safety googles from her hair. Then, setting down the eyewear, she caught herself pausing for a quick glance in the mirror.

Damn it.

Not allowing herself any time for primping, she went straight outside in time to see Vaughn open the door for his dog, leash in hand. Ruby hopped down the running board and onto the ground, wearing her service-dog vest.

"I hope it's not too late for a delivery," Vaughn

called, reaching into the truck to retrieve two brown paper bags. "I brought you some dinner for a bribe."

The bags were emblazoned with the logo for the Silver Saddle, the bar and tapas restaurant inside the Bellamy, Royal's new five-star resort. Abigail had never felt like she had the budget to indulge in any of the restaurants on the property, and her taste buds anticipated the treat as much as her rumbling stomach.

What a thoughtful gesture. Her heart squeezed tight to this new evidence of Vaughn's warmth and generosity.

"Since when do you need to bribe women into accepting gifts from you, Dr. Chambers?" she teased, hoping to keep things lighter between them as she stepped toward the truck bed and ran a hand over one of the gnarled pecan-tree branches. "I can't believe you loaded all of this up today. You must have been working since the moment I left your house."

"I didn't mind. It was a good day for a project." He paused as another, smaller pickup truck pulled in behind him, taking up all of Abigail's small driveway. More tree limbs spilled from the second cargo bed. "That's my groundskeeper's sons. They gave me a hand with it."

Overwhelmed at the thoughtfulness of the gesture, Abigail was having a hard time holding on to the boundaries she'd planned to draw. Especially as two grinning young men sprang from the second pickup, asking where to unload the limbs.

"This is Micah and Brandon." Vaughn made the introductions and let Abigail show the men where to lay the pieces, in a covered drying rack she'd built on the side of the house for that purpose.

"Should we give them a hand?" she asked him while the workers began unbuckling the harnesses on the first load.

Ruby stood at Vaughn's feet, watching along with them.

"Nah, we'd only get in their way. Those two are on a mission to earn extra cash for their own landscaping business." Vaughn shook his head with a laugh. "I can't keep them busy enough."

"I'm thrilled," she told him honestly, watching the drying rack begin to fill with pieces of wood for future projects. Regardless of the reservations she had about getting closer to Vaughn, she couldn't deny that he'd gone above and beyond to help her. "The installation at the hospital is really going to exhaust my store of raw materials, so this couldn't have come at a better time."

"My pleasure." His smile, when he chose to wield it, could melt polar ice caps. "And I hope you don't think it was presumptuous of me to bring dinner. Honestly, I was starving by the time we loaded up the trucks, and I figured you might be hungry, too, after all the time we spent outdoors today."

She wondered about that, sensing there might be more to it given the way he'd seemed to retreat after the kiss. Was this a simple olive branch to start over as friends? Or could that kiss have meant something more to him, too?

"I think it's very kind of you." Abigail hadn't eaten, either. She'd been too busy trying to distract herself from thoughts of the sexy doc by immersing herself in her work. Now, she couldn't help but think how much different her life would be if her baby had been fathered by someone like Vaughn. Someone thoughtful and caring. "After spending the first few months of my pregnancy feeling tired and depleted, my appetite has recently returned with a vengeance."

She figured it couldn't hurt to remind him of her baby, and where her allegiance would remain. She led him and Ruby through the house to the backyard patio, where a tiny flagstone courtyard was surrounded by plants and trees. While Vaughn began unboxing the meal, she retrieved plates and silverware from the house, along with cups and a pitcher of water. On her last trip, she remembered a bowl of water for Ruby and the matches for her outdoor lanterns.

A few minutes later, they sat across from one another at her wrought iron café table, enjoying the wealth of food Vaughn had provided. He'd moved one of her side tables from the porch down to the patio so they had more room. There were containers of bacon-wrapped dates, tiny crab empanadas, bruschetta with goat cheese and tomato, flatbreads with shrimp, crispy wonton chorizo ravioli and potato croquettes.

Vaughn had lit all four of the tiki torches filled with citronella oil to keep the mosquitoes away. The dancing flames combined with the feast made her feel like they were at a Hawaiian luau. She sat back in her seat, admiring the way the sky started to turn pink as the sun sank lower in the sky. The daylight lasted so long in the summer.

"That was fantastic," she declared, sipping her ice-cold water while Ruby sat beside Vaughn's chair.

"You didn't try these yet." Her dining companion passed a tray of more delicacies toward her. Tiny toasted puffs with a red sauce and a leafy green garnish.

"Everything is almost too pretty to eat." She reached for one anyhow, though. "What are they?"

"Cauliflower fritters with caviar." He lifted the water pitcher and refilled both their cups. "What do you think?"

A flutter in her belly made her smile, her hand reaching to cover the spot where she felt the phantom swirl of movement.

"I like it, and so does this baby." With each movement, her pregnancy became more real.

"You can tell?" Vaughn's expression shifted. Guarded, perhaps, but curious, too.

His interest touched her. She hadn't been able to share the joys of this pregnancy with anyone. Her mother made an effort to be excited, but she was still very mired in mourning Alannah, making Abigail less apt to share new developments.

So now, she pulled her chair closer to Vaughn's, wanting to share the wonder of something so miraculous. "May I have your hand?"

He swiped his fingers on a napkin, straightening in his chair before he rested his palm in hers. Abigail flipped it over so his hand faced down, then centered his touch high on her belly.

Warmth flooded her skin through her thin summer sheath dress. His large hand spanned her ribs, one finger trailing all the way to her navel, his thumb on her breastbone. Her mouth dried up, her heart pattering too fast, and he had to feel that. Memories of the kiss returned with new, heated intensity.

She lifted her gaze to his, losing the battle to maintain her defenses, wishing things could be different.

Then, the baby shifted.

A soft quiver of movement beneath his hand made his palm tense. Flex. His eyes went wide with a flicker of emotion.

"That's incredible." The awe in his voice made her remember why she'd wanted to share this with him.

It wasn't about getting closer to him, even though his touch made her feel breathless with awareness. She'd wanted him to feel the baby because that life inside her was special. Healing.

"Isn't it?" She let go of his fingers then, releasing him. "I haven't shared that with anyone." As soon as she said it, she realized how pathetic it sounded. "That is, my mother still lives in Austin and she's still working through her grief. So it's hard for her to be excited."

"I understand." Vaughn eased his hand away, but he rested it on the back of her chair, his fingers grazing her shoulder where the straps of her dress didn't quite cover. "It's only natural to want to celebrate something so profound. And while I'm sorry for your sake that Rich Lowell turned out to be a poor excuse for a man, I'm *not* sorry that his bad decisions gave me the chance to share something special with you."

Abigail held herself very still, knowing she needed to keep a rein on her runaway emotions. Vaughn was dealing with his own struggles—a serious disorder that might make a sufferer detach from all the things Abigail was feeling right now. So drawing him deeper into her world seemed unfair to him. To her. And to her baby.

Yet those wise intentions felt a world away with Vaughn by her side, his knuckle skimming her bare shoulder.

Mesmerized by his words, by the warmth in his green eyes, she couldn't think of a reply.

Just then, a rustle of movement and male laughter on the far side of the bungalow warned them of Vaughn's approaching workers.

"Dr. C." The taller of the pair, Micah, strode into the backyard first, holding up something shiny that glinted in the pink rays of the setting sun. "I wanted to deliver your extra set of truck keys before we take off. The wood is all stacked in the drying rack."

His brother trailed a few steps behind. Vaughn stood, thanking them both. Abigail used the moment to collect her thoughts. Give herself a mental shake. Standing, she began clearing the dishes, dismayed at how quickly sizzling attraction could stamp out good sense.

"I can help with that," Vaughn called, finishing up his conversation with the young men before covering the lawn with long strides so he could hold the back door open for her. Chivalrous. Thoughtful.

He brought Ruby with him to retrieve the rest of the leftovers from their meal and brought them to the door.

"Do you mind if she comes inside with me?" he asked. "I could set up a spot for her in the corner."

"Ruby is absolutely welcome indoors," Abigail assured him, making quick work of putting away the leftovers while Vaughn rinsed off the plates. "It's fun having her around."

She'd welcome a buffer of any sort if she was going to keep herself from swooning at Vaughn's feet again. Or outright requesting more kisses.

"Thank you." Closing the door behind him, he settled the dog in a quiet spot in the dining room, then began loading the flatware in the dishwasher. "Ruby has been good for me."

He glanced over at her where Ruby made herself comfortable with her head on her paws. See-ing the two of them together today—how bonded they were—made her think it must be difficult for Vaughn to be apart from her for his long hours at the hospital.

"She must miss you while you're working," she observed carefully, testing the waters on the topic. Wanting to know more about him. "I'm sure you put in long hours as a surgeon."

He placed the rest of the dishes inside the washer with the same methodical care before shutting the appliance door.

"The weeks where I'm on call are the toughest since I go in at all hours." He rinsed and dried his hands. Turned to watch her as she wiped down the small island countertop. "Micah and Brandon will take Ruby out if their father is busy with other things, so she's in good hands."

"I'm glad you have extra help. She doesn't go to the hospital?"

"There are plenty of jobs where service dogs are allowed, but ICU is a very different workplace."

"You must miss her, then." Setting aside the sponge, she rinsed her own hands then stood near him, where he leaned against the granite.

Her kitchen had never felt crowded before, but with a tall, sexy doctor beside her, dominating the space, she was all too aware of the tiny square footage.

"Surgery is my job." His jaw flexed, his gaze

fixed on a point beyond her shoulder. "It's the one thing I can perform no matter what else is going on around me."

If she'd missed the defensiveness in his voice, she sure would have seen it his tense arms. His rigid shoulders. Ruby must have felt the tension, too, since she rose from her seat to sit beside him, pressing her head against his thigh.

Okay.

Abigail had tested his comfort level regarding the challenges of his work environment, and found that was a do-not-cross line.

"That's another way our jobs are very different." Drying her hands, she retreated to a seat at one of the bar stools at the island. "Some days it feels like all the stars have to be in precise alignment for me to find the inspiration to create."

Rattling off a few of the things that could distract her when she was supposed to be working, Abigail was glad to see Vaughn's shoulders relax by degrees as she spoke. Even Ruby chilled out, going from a sitting position by Vaughn's knee to lying at his feet. Yet perhaps stepping on one of his personal land mines was a constructive reminder for her.

Vaughn Chambers was a magnetic man. Talented. Thoughtful. And charismatic when he wanted to be. But she couldn't allow herself to forget he wrestled demons in his spare time, and they weren't the kind that stepped aside to make room for a wishful heart like hers.

Five

Two nights later, Vaughn finished dictating his shift notes into his phone and sent them to transcription for updating his office files. Seated in a far corner of the nurses' station, he tuned out the noise around him. He'd already done rounds with the next critical-care team on duty, but inevitably he found a few additional thoughts cropping up before he left the hospital for the day. His knife-fight victim was recovering nicely, with no major organ involvement. There would be therapy for a sliced knee tendon and, later, elective surgery to repair a torn labrum in the right shoulder, a result of his attacker pinning his arm behind him. All things considered, the guy was damn lucky.

Vaughn, too. He hadn't lost a patient since returning from Afghanistan and wanted to keep it that way.

What he *hadn't* wanted was to advertise his emotional shortcomings to Abigail when he'd gone over
to her studio the other night. He'd planned to end
their day together on a high note by bringing her
the raw materials from his ranch—and some dinner,
too. Their kiss had played out so many times in his
memory that he found himself wanting more even
though everything in him warned that being with
her was going to be complicated.

So he'd gone over there and tried to keep things
light. Romantic, even.

It had been working, too. Conversation flowed
easily through a meal she clearly enjoyed. He'd been
relaxed and having a good time, too. Had sensed another kiss was imminent.

Then things took a downward turn when she
asked about Ruby and his job. He hadn't shared the
PTSD diagnosis with many people—period. So he
hadn't developed an ease with talking about it, which
must have come across in his surly response.

"Dr. Chambers, you're just the man I wanted to
see," a deep male voice greeted him, hauling Vaughn
out of his thoughts.

Troy "Hutch" Hutchinson was a maternal-fetal
specialist and a good friend. The guy was not only a
gifted doctor, but also a generous one, donating time
to Doctors Without Borders for a long stint in Africa.

Vaughn shoved out of the rolling chair at the nurses' station, clapping Hutch on the back. "Did you have time to look at the patient in 2C?"

He'd had a seventeen-year-old accident victim transferred from a rural hospital late in his shift. She hadn't required surgery, but her condition was critical, especially because of an early stage pregnancy.

"I just checked on your car-accident victim and her baby looks good." He laid a file folder on the nurses' station counter and helped himself to an apple from a gift fruit bowl delivered to the unit earlier in the day. "You up for tennis one of these days?"

Vaughn hadn't played in months, but he'd spoken to Hutch a few times about getting together to hit. The other man lived in Pine Valley, but he belonged to the Texas Cattleman's Club, too, so using the courts there presented no problem. Which brought to mind another question he had for his friend.

"I'm free all the time. *You're* the one with triplets." Vaughn remembered how happy the guy was when his wife, Simone, gave birth to three healthy babies.

"Right. And my serve is going to be rusty after devoting months to baby-rocking." He grinned between bites of apple. "Not that I'd trade the dad duty for anything. But if I don't stay in shape, I'm not going to be able to keep up when they start walking."

Vaughn wasn't so sure about that. Hutch was a gifted athlete at every sport and a prized teammate at any sports-related hospital charity event. But he wasn't going to argue. Vaughn needed to make an effort to reconnect with the world, as witnessed by his ineptitude making conversation with Abigail.

"Good point. Name the time and I'll be there." Pocketing his phone, Vaughn waved his colleague farther down the hall, away from beeping monitors and nurses buzzing in and out of the floor's hub. "I have a quick question for you first, if you have a minute."

"Sure thing." Hutch walked with him, tossing his apple core in a basket on the way.

They stopped by the window overlooking the top floor of the parking garage. The lights were on since it was after 9:00 p.m. and one car drew his eye in the mostly empty lot.

Abigail's compact vehicle was parked under one of the streetlamps. He recognized the vehicle from the magnet on one side, advertising her artwork. The knowledge that she was here, working late, sent a surge of longing through him. He wanted to see her.

Needed to see her.

"Hutch, I wasn't sure who else to ask about this..." Vaughn had put in a call to Will Sanders, hoping to learn more about possible danger to Abigail from the man who impersonated him. "But I've struck up a friendship with a woman who was involved with Will Sanders's imposter this winter."

"Rich Lowell." Hutch's lip curled, his disdain obvious.

"That's the name I heard, too. Is that confirmed?"

Vaughn hadn't gleaned much from Abigail the day he'd learned about her pregnancy, and he wanted to be sure she was safe. "Rich and Will used to be good friends."

"So I hear." Hutch leaned a shoulder against the window. He hadn't grown up in Royal, yet these days, he had a far better grasp on what was happening in town than Vaughn did. "But the police warned the TCC board to take extra precautions with any files Will had access to in the past year, including member profiles and sensitive data. Rich had access to everything."

"Do the police think he's still in the area?" Vaughn's gaze dropped to that solitary vehicle under the streetlamp again.

The nearest car was at least fifty yards away.

"They aren't ruling anything out. The FBI did DNA testing on the ashes that Jason Phillips shipped back after the plane crash that supposedly belonged to Will, and they definitely don't belong to Rich Lowell."

So Rich was alive. And a wanted felon.

"The guy could be dangerous." Vaughn's gut churned at the thought of Abigail being vulnerable to a man like that. He swore softly.

"I'm sure police have warned her to be careful. They've spoken to everyone who was close to the imposter." Hutch straightened from where he leaned against the window, his phone vibrating in his pocket. "And I hear Will is hiring a private detective to do some work on the case, too. Make sure nothing gets overlooked."

Hutch checked his message while Vaughn plotted the fastest path to the children's ward. He had to check on Abigail. An artist living alone in a downtown bungalow didn't have the resources that someone like Will did. She couldn't hire her own investigator or a bodyguard.

"Thanks for the update." Vaughn backed away, thinking the stairs were quickest. "And I'm not letting you off the hook for tennis."

Hutch grinned as he pocketed his phone. "You think I'm beatable after a few months away from my game?"

"No one's reign lasts forever." He levered open the door to the stairwell and headed down a flight to the children's ward, where Abigail must still be working.

He hadn't wanted to push for more with her when his head was wrecked and she was expecting another man's child. She had a lot on her plate, and so did he. But if she was in danger, all bets were off.

He would make damn sure he was there to keep her safe.

The tree needed more branches.

Abigail could appreciate that now that she saw the tree sculpture in its new home in the Royal Memorial Hospital children's ward. Art took on a different appearance according to the surroundings—the light, the space, the colors nearby. And after paying a professional mover to relocate her half-finished piece this afternoon, she could see that she had more work left to do than she had imagined.

She didn't mind the extra effort. This project meant so much to her that she wanted it to be perfect. Abigail liked the idea of a tree with deep roots and extensive branches that reached out to draw in visitors. A place of comfort and reflection.

What Abigail *did* mind was the added expense of paying a mover to transport more raw materials to the hospital. If she'd been thinking ahead, she could have saved herself some money by incorporating everything she needed into one trip. Considering how long that commission check needed to last her, it was essential to start making smarter decisions to spend wisely.

She took out a pen and paper from her purse to write notes about which pieces would fit the sculpture best to add new branches to the tree. Then, lowering herself to the work platform she'd installed around the base of the tree, she tucked a foot beneath her and started a list.

The lounge was quiet tonight, making it easy to concentrate. When the sculpture was finished, the lounge would extend to the area around her tree, but for now, the hospital building crew had roped off her job site. It didn't stop interested people from hopping over to take a peek or offer a compliment, but it wasn't as though she had to work with many people around her.

By tomorrow, there would be plastic sheeting hung up all around the sculpture so she could use her electric tools. For now, she scribbled.

She was so lost in thought, imagining a pattern of wood pieces grafted to the central trunk, that she never heard footsteps approach. She startled when a man's voice intruded on her note-taking.

"It's awfully late for you to be here." Vaughn stood close to the platform, dressed in street clothes—khaki-colored pants and a white button-down with a necktie that could have been a postmodern painting. A few splashes of color on a black field.

Her heart warmed to see him in spite of all her stern warnings to keep her distance. The tone of his voice skimmed her senses like a caress, hitting all the right places and making her think about kissing him again. It wasn't fair to feel so physically aware of him when she knew he might not be in a position for a relationship, battling his PTSD issues so hard. But she hadn't even opened her mouth to speak and she was already tingling with sensual want.

"I had to move the tree trunk into place today so I can do more of the carving on site." She shuffled aside her notebook and pen. "There comes a point in the process where it becomes risky to move the statue if I've already done a lot of detail work."

"I could have helped you." He stared up at the trunk and the preliminary branches—mostly raw, uncarved wood in bay laurel to match the trunk.

"How did you get it all over here?" He lowered his voice for her ears alone. "You need to be careful while you're pregnant."

"I am. I hired a moving company." She ran her hand up one side of the tree where she'd done a little craving today, notching out some thick bark for texture. Better to touch the tree than the man who tempted her. "And I would have hired your groundskeeper's sons since they were so helpful with stacking the new wood, but I booked the movers the day I got the commission."

"It looks great." He pointed to a carved creature already hiding inside a hollow. "I really like the barn owl."

She flushed with pleasure at the compliment. "Thank you. I hope to add quite a few birds." Her birds were popular in the local antiques-and-crafts store, Priceless, where she sold a few of her works. "Although I'm not sure how many I will finish before the summer gala since I've realized I want the scale to be bigger."

"It's already huge." Vaughn stepped up on the platform and stretched his arms around the trunk as far as they would go. Less than half way around. "Are you sure?"

"Definitely." She flipped her notepad up to him so he could see what she'd drawn. "I started making a list of what I want to bring over here, but I ended up making a sketch of the revised branch scheme."

"I like it." He nodded, peering up from the sketch

to the sculpture in progress. "But how will you notch in all those new branches?"

"That part will be time-consuming," she admitted. "And since it involves technical craftsmanship as opposed to artistry that will show in the final product, it's the kind of thing I could hire out if I knew someone skilled in carving."

Like furniture making, grafting on the branches involved making seamless joints. Fitting pegs into perfectly cut slots.

"I'll find someone who can help you." He shifted to sit down beside her on the platform.

His knee brushed hers, the touch sending ripples of awareness along her skin far beyond the point of contact. She'd worn a T-shirt with the simple cotton A-line skirt, a good uniform for a job site since it was comfortable enough while still appearing professional. The lightweight cotton wasn't much of a barrier for her leg next to his strong thigh. Her throat dried up and she took an extra moment to steel herself against the feel of him.

"That's all right, Vaughn. I told the art committee that I could finish this project in the allotted time frame, and I will. It just means a few more late nights." Possibly it meant seeing the handsome doctor a few more times, too.

What woman didn't enjoy being around a man who made her heart beat faster? Even if he should be off-limits?

"I want to talk to you about that." His voice was quiet again. Serious. "Have the police spoken to you about taking extra precautions now that they believe Rich Lowell is still alive?"

She hadn't expected this line of conversation at all. And although she'd been warned to keep the details of the investigation quiet, she guessed Vaughn probably knew more about it than her, considering his TCC connections.

Following his lead, she kept her voice quiet as well, needing to keep the conversation confidential. There was one young couple in the waiting lounge nearby. The woman read a book while the husband snoozed on her shoulder.

"I got a call from a federal agent last week." She hadn't known what to make of it at the time. Because as much as she resented Will Sanders's impersonator, she was unclear how much of a threat he posed to her and the rest of Royal. Yes, he was a horrible person, but she wasn't sure if he was outright dangerous to her. "She told me the remains delivered for Will Sanders's funeral did not match Rich's DNA and that investigators had every reason to believe he was alive."

"I heard." Vaughn's green eyes locked on hers, his expression grim. "Didn't she tell you to be more careful? What if he tries to contact you?"

At the time of the phone call, Abigail had just read a letter from her mortgage company threatening to start foreclosure proceedings if she missed another month's payment, so she may not have been as focused as she should have been.

Her life was so far from where she wanted it to be for her child. Guilt nipped. She touched her expanding belly, the smooth curve of new life more evident when she was seated.

"The agent told me not to reach out to him. And asked again if I had any idea of his whereabouts." She shook her head, remembering all the times she'd been asked that same question. How sad for her child's sake that the man she'd been involved with was on the run from the authorities, a completely inappropriate choice for a partner that would follow her forever. "I told her absolutely not and that I wouldn't try to contact him again if I did."

"But you're carrying his child." His hand went to her knee. A gesture of emphasis, perhaps.

Yet the warmth of his palm lying lightly on her thigh sent a shiver of pleasure through her.

"He doesn't know that."

Vaughn's eyebrows lifted, his hand sliding away. "You never told him?"

Her skin still felt warm where his hand had been.

"He was hardly in town this spring." She had felt guilty about her lack of communication at first. But once she'd discovered how deep his deception went, she was actually relieved. "Earlier this year, he was flying back and forth to Ireland. Then he was out of the country on business. Finally, I went to the main house once to try to speak to him."

Overhead on the PA system, a doctor was paged, the announcement blaring into their corner of the hospital, which was otherwise so quiet.

"When was that?" Vaughn asked when the speaker went quiet again.

She thought back. "The first week of May, maybe?" So much had happened in the last few months. "It was probably a week before the plane crash. Maybe a little less."

"And Rich wasn't at the Ace in the Hole that day?"

"I have a hard time thinking of him as Rich." She had never even met Richard Lowell, as himself—he was a man others in Royal knew well enough for his friendship with Will. "Don't forget, I thought Rich was dead in a boating accident and that Will had moved on after losing his closest friend." Her chest hurt remembering their conversation about that. "He told me about that accident on the night—on Alannah's birthday. When I was falling apart and feeling vulnerable. He made me feel like we were kindred souls, mourning people we loved."

Bitterness gave the words a bad taste. The more that came to light about Rich Lowell's deceptions, the more she realized how thoroughly she'd been played. He had taken advantage of her grief, maneuvering her right where he wanted her.

And she'd been too caught up in her own loss to notice.

"The bastard."

Vaughn's quiet assessment of the situation mirrored her own.

"My thought exactly. But on that day, when I went to the main house on the ranch to confront him, he was there." She had been prepared to bargain for full custody. Offer to move out of town even, if that would help Will, since he'd never left his wife even though he'd told her that he and Megan were separated. Abigail had hoped he would want nothing to do with the baby. "I went in the back way, toward the office where I had done temp work. The desk and room where I used to work was empty, but I could hear arguing in Will's—er, Rich's—private office."

"Do you think it was Rich's voice?" Vaughn's hand shifted to rest lightly between her shoulder blades.

She realized then how wrong her first impression of him had been. That he was an arrogant. Brash and blunt. Since that first meeting he demonstrated a tenderness and empathy for her that made her understand what made him a good doctor. His patients must feel well cared for.

"I know it was Rich because I peeked inside the office door. It was open a crack." She'd been startled by what she saw. A very different side of the man who'd been her boss for two months. "Just as I reached the door, to see who he was arguing with, there was a thumping noise. Like a shove or a punch. And when I looked inside, Rich was fighting with Jason Phillips."

Vaughn swore. "Jason Phillips? The same man who sent the urn back with Will's remains, only they weren't Will's remains."

Jason, like Will, was also a member of the Texas Cattleman's Club. He was a key player at Will's energy company, Spark Energy Solutions, although Abigail didn't remember his exact role. He lived part-time in Dallas and part-time in Royal. She'd never heard him speak an angry word before that day she'd seen him fighting with the man who was impersonating Will.

"Is Jason a suspect in stealing from Will? Or do they think he knew that Rich Lowell was a fake?"

A cleaning crew rolled a cart past the lounge, mops and cleaners rattling as they steered their supplies over a threshold. The two women pushing it were having a rapid disagreement about whose turn it was to use the floor-polishing machine. The argument faded along with the clacking of the cart's wheels.

Vaughn tracked their progress, waiting until it was quiet again before he answered. "I've heard Jason is away on international business and can't be reached. He could be Rich's accomplice. He could have double-crossed him. Or he could have been completely innocent and his only crime was figuring out that Rich was a thief. But I think it's clear you walked in on a very dangerous situation that day."

At the time, she simply didn't want to be around men who were fighting. She didn't want her baby around violence, either. But maybe she'd escaped something much worse. A new wariness crept over her, making her grateful for Vaughn coming here tonight. For checking on her.

A chill had taken hold of her while they spoke. And the only place that felt warm was the spot where Vaughn touched. His hand still rested between her shoulders, as he continued to rub lightly.

Unable to resist the comfort he offered, she tipped her head onto his shoulder. Allowed herself to soak in the feel of his arm tightening around her, hugging her close. For the moment, she felt safe. Protected.

"I don't think Rich Lowell would come after me." She would be more careful anyhow, of course. "He doesn't know I'm carrying his child, and he would be wise to stay far away from Royal with everyone looking for him." If he'd stolen as much money from the real Will as she'd heard, he would be able to start a new life somewhere far, far away.

Vaughn turned more fully toward her, taking her shoulders in his hands so he could look into her eyes. "He might not come for his child, Abigail. But what if he knows you saw him fighting with Jason? What if you saw or heard something significant that day without realizing it?"

Fear sank deep inside her. She swayed slightly, and Vaughn reached to steady her. "But I didn't hear anything specific. I don't know what they were arguing about. I just recognized angry voices."

"I believe you, honey. And I'm not trying to frighten you. But I can't stress enough how important it is for you to be careful." He smoothed a path down her shoulders to her upper arms. "Have Security walk you out to your car at night. Install an alarm system at home and make sure you use it. But most of all, we need to call the police and let them know you saw Rich and Jason fighting."

Her mind whirled. Of course, he was right about all of those things. She wasn't just protecting herself. She needed to make sure her child was safe. And for that reason, she would part with the extra money for an alarm system, even though it would put a bigger dent in that commission check.

"I will." Nodding, she tried not to feel overwhelmed. But her plate had been full before with a baby on the way and a massive art project to complete. Now, installing a new system would take time. And how could she compare prices when she felt like she needed protection right now? "I can stop by the station tonight on the way home."

She could cross that much off her list anyhow, even though she was bone-weary.

"It's already late. You must be exhausted." He studied her for a long moment.

She could tell he was thinking. And how funny that she'd known him for such a short time and already she understood things like that about him.

"It's not a problem. If I had any idea that what I'd seen was significant, I would have reported it already." Shoving her notepad and drawings in her purse, she prepared to leave the hospital. "I'd better get underway, though. I want to be here early tomorrow to put in a full day's work."

"May I make a suggestion?" He waited for her nod. "I don't want to impose, but I'm happy to help."

He drew a breath, ready to roll out some kind of plan, but she shook her head.

"No. You've already done so much to help me. Just giving me this commission in the first place—"

"I didn't do that for you. That was your talent. You were the committee's first choice."

She wondered if that carefully worded answer meant that he hadn't voted for her project. Not that it mattered. She'd gotten the job that meant everything to her. "Then you helped me by giving me access to your ranch and delivering all those tree limbs that will fuel my art for a long time to come."

Sliding off the work platform she'd built around her sculpture, she hopped to her feet. Searched in her bag for her keys.

"My landscaper would have only created a burn pile with them otherwise. Giving them to you saves us the trouble." He stood with her, stilling her hands before she could tug her keys from her purse. "Abigail, there are four empty bedrooms at my ranch. Sleep there tonight where you have Ruby and me to watch over you. Then, we can have a squad car come out tomorrow to talk to you there. You'll get a good night's rest and then can give a statement in the morning."

Vaughn's hands held hers. Their gazes locked. Her throat went dry.

"Sleep...at your place?" Her voice scratched over the words a little, the invitation making her think all the wrong things.

All the things she'd been trying not to picture happening between her and the most appealing man she'd ever met.

"Sleep," he repeated, voice firm. "Trust me, I understand how the last guy you were with took advantage. I would never hurt you that way, swooping in to capitalize on a vulnerable moment."

Oh. She nodded stiffly, thinking it was probably a very sound plan. A wise idea. Good, rational thinking to help a pregnant woman get her rest and keep her safe.

"Thank you. If you don't mind, I will take you up on that." She liked the idea of having Vaughn by her side when she gave her statement to the police. For his friendship. His support. And yes, the tender concern he'd showed her. She couldn't deny that he was coming to mean a great deal to her.

"Good. I can drive you there." He checked his watch. "I'll have to be to work early in the morning, too, so we can ride in together." He walked her out to her car, stopping there just long enough so she could get a few of her things and lock it up again for the night.

And then he was on the phone with the Royal police—a call to someone on the force he went to school with, apparently—and arranged for an officer to come out in the morning. It was all helpful and logical. Kind and thoughtful.

Yet, as she slid into the passenger seat of the sexy sports car he used for work, Abigail couldn't help but wish that Vaughn didn't feel the need to be quite so honorable where she was concerned. She wasn't all that vulnerable, damn it.

If she wanted something more to happen between them, she was definitely in full command of her senses to make the decision. Not like that awful night back in February.

No one was taking advantage of her again.

A part of her wanted to plot a way to kiss him senseless as soon as they walked into his house. But the part of her that was five months pregnant reminded her she needed to think like a mother and not a woman with a fierce hunger for the man in the driver's seat.

Just sleep? She feared she was going to be too hot and bothered to even close her eyes.

Six

Vaughn wasn't the only one excited to have a visitor. Ruby greeted Abigail with the full-on joy of the dog's off-duty personality. A happy, panting, tail-wagging, follow-Abigail-everywhere welcome. As grateful as Vaughn was for the service animal's training, he liked seeing the golden retriever simply enjoy their guest while he helped her settle into a downstairs bedroom. Abigail, for her part, seemed equally charmed. She had laughed with delight to see one of Ruby's unsung skills on display as the dog helped her "unpack." Abigail had brought a gym bag that she'd retrieved from her own car, a duffel she kept with clean clothes, a towel and toiletries.

When Ruby sat at Abigail's feet as she opened the

bag, Vaughn mentioned Ruby's unique gift. Only when Abigail clamored to see did he give Ruby the command to unpack, and the dog carefully gripped the toiletry bag in her teeth, carrying it to a drawer Vaughn had opened for her. One by one, Ruby transplanted all the items in the duffle.

"She's amazing," Abigail proclaimed while Vaughn rewarded her with a treat and released her to play.

Even then, Ruby didn't venture far, wandering in and out of the suite while Vaughn double-checked that the room and attached bath had fresh towels and linens. Did the dog sense he needed a chaperone? He'd given Abigail his word that his offer for her to stay here was just to help her and keep her safe at a juncture in her life that had to be incredibly challenging. So, of course, Vaughn wasn't going to let himself linger in this room with her for long. He would keep his word. But he wouldn't court temptation, either.

The room he'd given her was spacious, with three walls painted in a soft tan, while the wall behind the dark wood headboard was lined with reclaimed planks, like an old barn. A giant pair of steer horns had been mounted above the bed.

"Can I get you anything else?" he asked after assuring himself she had clean towels. He stalked back into the bedroom, where she sat on the black painted chest at the end of the sleigh bed.

A stack of extra blankets rested beside her, not that she'd need them in July, but he'd wanted to make sure she was comfortable. She'd kicked off the pink tennis shoes she had worn with her gray floral skirt and T-shirt, the pink canvas a feminine touch in a room otherwise full of heavy, dark woods and Aztec-themed patterns in the rugs, pillows and prints on the wall.

"You've already been so generous." Abigail stroked Ruby's silky ears while the dog rested her head on the chest beside their guest.

"A bottle of water? A snack before bed?" He knew he should let her sleep, but he also wouldn't deny a pregnant woman sustenance. "I didn't have much time for dinner, so I'm going to make something for myself."

Pulling her attention from his adoring dog, Abigail met his gaze slowly. There was something different in her expression. A determination, maybe. Or certainty.

"I'm hungry, too." She tilted her chin up as she came to her feet. Her skirt settled around her knees in a swirl of cotton knit. "Just not that kind of hungry."

He stilled. His heartbeat stuttered as his brain tried to take in the words and what they meant. Behind her, Ruby curled at the end of the chest. Content.

Clearly, his dog wasn't worried about whatever was happening here. But Vaughn wasn't so sure about himself.

"I brought you here to make life easier for you," he reminded her, remembering what she'd been through with Rich Lowell. "I don't want to take advantage of you on a day when you've had a scare. When the world is off-kilter."

He wanted to place his hands on her as she stepped closer to him. Comfort and reassure her. But with the sultry look in her eyes, he didn't fully trust himself. The heat that had been simmering between them threatened to bubble over at the least provocation.

"My world is not off-kilter." She halted just inches away from him in the center of the room, under the ceiling fan that spun silently on a low setting, the air teasing through her dark curls. She lifted both hands to his chest and placed them there. "I wanted to be here tonight, not just to be safe from the past. But maybe to erase some of it, too."

Her fingers stroked along his shirt, smoothing either side of the placket. The citrus-and-spice scent of her fragrance teased his nose. Memories of her taste threatened to level all his good intentions.

Heat rushed up his spine.

"Abigail." He held her shoulders, needing to keep her still another moment while he wrapped his brain around this. "I like you. Too damn much. I would never want you to regret this."

"The last time for me was so emotionally painful," she confided, her dark eyes wide. Sincere. "I was vulnerable and weak. Now, I'm sure of myself. And I understand this isn't necessarily going to lead to anything. I know you aren't ready for a relation-ship. I just—" She shook her head, brow furrowed.

"What?" His voice was ragged with need, but he tipped his chin up to see her more clearly. Wanting to understand.

"I want a beautiful memory to replace an unhappy one."

The certainty in her voice broke through his last restraint.

He wanted her more than he could remember ever wanting a woman before. She understood he couldn't offer forever. But he could damn well give her this.

"Then I'm going to make that happen, Abigail." He skimmed a touch around her waist, his hands ach-ing for a better feel of her. "Tonight, we're going to torch those old memories for good."

Breathless, Abigail was glad Vaughn held on to her because her knees went liquid at his promise.

She'd made her desire plain. Taken control of her wants. And this incredibly sexy man pledged to de-liver all of it. She shivered with longing as his hands spanned her hips, pulling her to him.

He felt strong. Immovable. His body was a tes-tament to physical training. Yet he'd been so tender with his kiss in the woods. So thoughtful with her tonight.

Now, she wanted all that delicious male muscle around her. Enveloping her. Holding her. She arched up on her toes and kissed him, the scruff of beard a gentle abrasion to her chin and cheeks, depending how she shifted against him. For a moment, she breathed him in. The scent of woodsy soap and musky man, the sensual glide of his tongue along her lower lip.

Teasing, tempting, tasting.

Then, the kiss went a little wild. A groan of hunger from him. A sigh of pleasure from her. Fingers combing through his thick hair, she couldn't feel enough of him. She kissed a path along his cheek and his jaw, her body melting everywhere he touched her. Her dress felt paper-thin, the heat of his body setting hers aflame.

He walked them backward toward the bed, falling with her onto the king-size mattress, taking her weight so she settled gently into the soft red duvet printed with a gray-and-white Aztec design.

"Are you okay?" Vaughn asked, a soft whisper in her ear. "I want to be careful with you."

His teeth nipped the tender lobe, sending a quiver down her spine. Her hair spilled all around them, some of the curls still clinging to his shoulders as he angled back to unfasten her skirt.

"I'm perfect." She reached to work on the buttons on his shirt, wanting to feel his skin without any barrier. "I want more. I want to see you."

His green eyes tracked hers, thoughtfully assessing. Or maybe seeing how serious she was about that.

"That feeling is mutual." He raised up on his elbow, then all the way to a sitting position. "But since tonight is all about you, I'll go first."

"Slowly," she blurted. Because she was having such an incredible track record with getting what she wanted tonight she might as well go for broke.

A darkly masculine smile made her feel faint with yearning. But he unfastened one button after another. Taking his time. "I like this sensual streak I'm beginning to see."

She tugged a pillow under her head to make herself more comfortable, watching his talented hands work. "I'm an artist, remember? I have a fondness for appealing lines and angles."

Stripping off his dress shirt, he wore a fitted white tank beneath it. He reached behind him to tug that over his head, tossing both onto the chest at the foot of the sleigh bed.

Vaughn clothed was a sight to behold.

Vaughn with no shirt was a vision of athletic male grace. Tattoos swirled and danced on his collarbone and chest. Tribal art in black work, she thought at first. But as she looked closer there were names inked into those graphic swirls. Dates.

Her heart squeezed in recognition. Understanding.

He was covered with a vibrant pattern of losses.

She didn't need to ask to know. Shifting to her knees, she leaned closer to kiss the places where

Vaughn had etched a memorial to patients, maybe, and to the brothers lost in Afghanistan.

Too many.

For a moment, he allowed the gentle tribute of her lips on his skin, combing his fingers through her tousled hair. But then he edged away to meet her gaze.

"Do I get to see you now?" His hands bracketed her hips, thumbs retreating just a little way under the hem of her T-shirt, where he touched bare skin.

He sought to redirect her, she thought, unwilling to share stories about those names on his body. She understood about sharing loss in small doses. Understood how much it could hurt.

So she let him set the pace where his past was concern. Instead, she focused on his thumbs grazing her expanding waist, his touch causing delicious shivers. Pleasure coursed through her veins, thick and hot.

With it, however, came a hint of reservation.

"My body isn't the stuff of male fantasy these days," she reminded him, sinking back on her heels a bit.

"You, of all people, must know how thoroughly pregnant bodies have captivated the artistic imagination for centuries." He molded his hands to her body under her shirt, feeling the curve of her stomach and hips. "A woman is never more beautiful than when she's carrying a new life inside her."

Her throat burned a little at his sweet words. And gave her the courage to strip off her gray T-shirt, revealing her pink satin bra, a splurge she'd made with the commission check to accommodate her newly generous breasts.

"Slowly," he reminded her, his gaze fixed on her body, his voice rougher than it was a moment before. "I have a fondness for curves."

A smile pulled at her lips. She raised up on her knees again, confidence renewed. She flicked open the clasp on the bra, letting the cups part so she could shrug off the straps.

"So beautiful." The whispered reverence inflamed her skin just before he kissed one tight peak. Chased a circle around the center with his tongue.

Her body ached for him with a new, heightened need. Heat pooled between her thighs and she pressed herself tighter to him, wanting more.

She let her hands roam all over him, tracing the ridges of muscle and exploring the dips and hollows that came with them. She felt the hiss of breath between his teeth as he switched from one breast to the other, drawing on her harder, taking her fully into his mouth.

Allowing her hands to wander lower, she skimmed the intriguing planes of his abs before she ran into his belt. With impatient fingers, she made quick work of the buckle, the hook, the zipper.

And stroked a touch up the proud, thrusting length of him.

The guttural sound he made echoed the rough

want she was feeling. She needed him inside her. Moving with her. Filling her.

But he clamped her hand in his, halting her touch before she peeled away his boxers.

"It's been a long time for me." His green eyes were stark with need. A sheen of sweat glistened on his forehead that hadn't been there a moment ago.

She kissed his cheek. Licked along his lower lip. "Me, too."

"Give me a minute." He slid off the bed and stepped out his clothes, leaving him gloriously naked.

With all the lights on in her room, she could see every perfect inch of him as he retreated into another room, returning a few moments later with a condom in hand.

At least, she thought that's what he flashed at her when he entered the room, but she was still plenty distracted by the sight of him naked. Never taking her eyes off him, she stood to let her undone skirt fall on the ground. Then, tucking her thumbs in the waistband of her pink satin bikini underwear, she lowered those, too.

"You are the prettiest thing I've ever seen, Abigail." He left the condom on the bed and cupped the back of her neck, hauling her close to kiss her. Then lowered her ever so gently to the bed.

He stretched out on top of her, the warm brush of hair on his leg a tickle against her smooth one. Her breasts molded to his chest. His erection a hot, silken weight pressing between her thighs.

He kissed her then, and things got serious. Awed. Humbled. Reverent. Wordlessly, she rolled on top of him, wanting to see him better. Needing to take ownership of this moment. This incredible night.

His thigh parted hers, a welcome pressure and heat to fill the ache that grew worse by the second. She fumbled with the condom, ready for everything.

She whispered his name, needing him now. He took the packet and finished opening it, sheathing himself while she kissed his chest. Lower.

"Abby." He breathed the nickname into her hair as he hauled her up his body again.

Then he came inside her, inch by inch, until her eyes fluttered closed against the bliss of it. She felt the slick perfection of it all the way to her toes. Her head lolled forward, resting on his chest for a long moment until she gathered herself. Moved her hips.

His groan of satisfaction spread through her, vibrating inside her. This time, when he rolled her to her back, she let him, ready to relinquish that control since hers was ready to shatter. She was close to release, and they'd only just started, her body starved for all that he could do to her. For her. With her.

She knew once with Vaughn would never be enough.

Meeting his green gaze, she watched him moving over her. Mesmerized.

Once, he leaned down to whisper her name in her ear, reaching between their bodies to pluck gently at the tender core of her. She flew apart instantly, wave after wave of pleasure breaking over her, drowning her in the sweetest release.

In the middle of it, she opened her eyes just enough to see him watching her. She found just enough wherewithal to lift her hips, taking him deeper. And in that moment, his body tensed. Spasmed. His own completion rocked him as every muscle went rigid.

They held each other for long moments afterward. At some point, he'd pulled one of the spare blankets over them while the overhead fan turned lazily above. At the foot of the bed, Ruby still snoozed, the occasional dog snuffle and sigh a reminder of her presence.

Abigail felt a beautiful languidness in her limbs. She lay her head on Vaughn's chest after they'd disentangled themselves. She hoped he wouldn't regret this night together. She understood he wasn't ready for a relationship.

Knew that he struggled to make emotional connections because of the disorder he battled. Of course it would be daunting for him to be involved right now.

And yet, a little part of her couldn't help thinking they'd taken a step forward together in spite of everything. He'd admitted he hadn't been with anyone else in a long time, making her think this had been special for him, too.

As exhaustion pulled her toward sleep after an eventful day, Abigail told herself not to read too much into what had just happened. She had only just begun to truly heal from her sister's death. From the devastation of learning her baby's father was an imposter, a thief and a possible threat to her.

She couldn't afford another hit this year.

Where Vaughn was concerned, hope might be a dangerous emotion.

Seven

Vaughn lay awake in the spare bedroom beside Abigail well past midnight, hating to leave her side too soon after the way the father of her child had checked out on her.

He liked being here, brushing touches over her hair while she slept. Seeing a hint of a smile curve her lips, welcoming his touch.

But falling asleep beside her meant the possibility of nightmares, and he didn't want to freak her out if that happened. Granted, the nightmares had decreased since Ruby came along. The dog was aces when it came to sensing trouble at night. She nuzzled his arm or his face, whimpering until he awoke. She usually alerted him before things took a turn for the terrifying. But if Ruby knew to rouse him, that was because he was already making noise or starting to wrestle the blankets. He'd disturb Abigail for sure.

So he laid there, contemplating his next move.

Sex had been amazing. Far more than a simple release, their time together had rocked him. He hadn't expected to be so thoroughly captivated by her. Or touched by the fact that she'd chosen him to help her erase her demons. That alone had been an unanticipated gift.

As for all the rest? He was still blown away hours later.

Tomorrow, he would stay by her side while she gave a statement to the police. He planned to place another call to Will Sanders to give the guy an update since—if their roles were reversed—Vaughn sure as hell would want to know about Rich fighting with Jason Phillips in his office. The information had to be significant.

And the more he thought about it, bad news for Jason. The last guy to get on the wrong side of Rich was Will himself. Will had paid for that by having his identity—and months of his life—stolen from him. Considering no one could reach Jason to speak with him personally, that didn't bode well for him.

Vaughn also wanted to find some skilled help for Abigail to work on the sculpture so she didn't exhaust herself during her pregnancy. He'd already asked Micah to meet them at her place in the morning. Abigail wanted to stop by her house before they continued to the hospital, and Vaughn figured Micah could either use the pickup to haul her extra wood pieces to the hospital, or he could help dig the ditch around her house to facilitate the alarm system she needed.

Actually, now that he thought about it, Micah better bring Brandon with him to get everything done. Vaughn scheduled a text to hit their phones tomorrow morning at six so they could plan their workday accordingly.

But if he wanted any sleep tonight for a full day ahead, he needed to retreat to his own room, behind a closed door. Sliding out of bed, Vaughn figured he would simply set an alarm to wake early and start breakfast. Maybe Abigail would never notice he'd left her side.

Calling softly to Ruby, he headed toward the door. He wasn't going to scare a pregnant woman with the hell that played out behind his closed eyes on a nightly basis. Which already had him wondering, how long would she be content to spend time with a shell of a man who had so little of himself to give?

After she'd given a statement to police the next morning, Abigail rode in the passenger seat of Vaughn's truck on the way to the hospital.

They were stopping at her house first, to pick up a few extra tools she needed and so she could change into something more work appropriate than the yoga pants and T-shirt she kept in her gym bag.

Despite the incredible night with Vaughn—a night she refused to regret—she had awoken alone. The sheets were cold on his side of the bed, too, so it wasn't as though he'd been beside her recently. She'd smelled breakfast cooking, however, so that had been thoughtful of him. But the aftermath of their intimacy had been awkward. She felt him pulling back. And while she wasn't surprised, given what she knew about him and his past, she couldn't deny feeling the sting of his retreat.

Plucking at her shirt, she tried not to think about the events of the past day with Vaughn. The morning was already relentlessly hot, the humidity thick and heavy just outside the air-conditioning of his truck. Awareness of the man beside her—and the nerve-racking mess of her past—made her skin burn all the more.

"Officer Grant made it sound like I would be questioned again about the fight I witnessed, didn't he?" She thought back to the early morning visit from Vaughn's friend in the Royal Police Department, a higher-ranking police official who rode over to the ranch along with a uniformed officer.

"With the FBI involved, they must be looking at a lot of different facets of crimes committed," Vaughn noted, his phone vibrating with incoming messages while they sat at a traffic light.

Her stomach cramped in visceral response to his words. How was it possible that she'd been involved with a man wanted for questioning by both of those federal agencies? Her life had turned strange and scary in the past few months, and she couldn't deny that she felt grateful for Vaughn sitting beside her now. And this morning, too, while she gave her statement to his police-officer friend.

She knew she couldn't depend on the handsome doc long-term, but for now, she distracted herself by glancing over at him. He wore a light gray button-down this morning along with gray dress pants and a pair of dark leather loafers with subtle stitch work on the toes that looked handmade.

She'd noticed that about his home, too. He must support private craftsmen with his purchases because he didn't own the kind of expensive items that filled high-end stores. She'd looked over the Aztec blankets in her room this morning—when she'd awoken alone—and saw they were sewn by hand and not a machine. They were high quality, of course. But definitely crafted by artisans.

That was different from the way Will—that is, Rich Lowell—had thrown money around. He used it to show his status, flashing cash as if there was an unending supply. Vaughn, on the other hand, while clearly well-off through his family's wealth above and beyond his thriving practice, seemed to understand that the culture was richer for spending

money on the arts. Those funds supported people
who wanted to beautify and better the world, people
who protected the old ways of doing things so they
wouldn't be forgotten in the rush to mechanize and
outsource everything.

"I think you'll be telling the story again," Vaughn
agreed as they neared downtown. His shirt stretched
around his broad shoulders and muscular upper
arms. The cuffs were still rolled from when he'd
made them breakfast—huevos rancheros with Tex-
Mex flair. "If not to the FBI, then Will's private investigator might want to hear it."

She sighed. As nice as it had been to awaken to
breakfast already made for her, she would have pre-
ferred to feel his arms around her instead.

"I just hope they find Rich soon." She didn't want
these worries hanging over her head when her baby
was born.

"They will." He sounded so certain. "Investigators are throwing too much firepower at this for it to
drag out." He rolled to a stop sign and glanced over
at her. "But in the meantime, I'd like to give you—
and your child—a gift that should help you feel more
secure at home."

She frowned as he turned town her street. At the
far end, in front of her bungalow, she recognized the
older model pickup truck that his workers had driven
over before. It sat in her driveway now.

"I don't understand." She straightened in her seat,

trying to see what Vaughn had in mind. "You aren't responsible for us, Vaughn. There's no need—"

"I know that. I want to help. Consider it an early baby-shower gift." He slowed to a stop behind the red Ford. "At first, I asked Micah and Brandon to meet us here in case you needed help bringing raw material to the hospital." He put his own pickup in Park and switched off the engine while both of his workers hopped out of their vehicle. "But then, I thought it would be a good idea for them to bring some shovels so they could lay the wire for a home security system I'm having installed."

He'd arranged all of that? Stunned, it took her a moment to reply.

"That's far too generous. I can't let you do that." Being independent meant making wise financial decisions on a budget. She could put it on an installment plan.

"You can pay the monitoring fee." He offered that like it was a compromise. "But for today, we'll at least get you up and running so you can sleep here tonight."

Outside on her lawn, she could see the brothers taking measurements of her front yard, stretching a metal tape between them. She let Vaughn's words roll around her brain, trying not to overreact to the implication that she wouldn't be welcome at Vaughn's house on a regular basis. Was she reading too much into it?

Or was that an astute assessment based on how he'd left her bed after their night together?

"In that case, because I wouldn't want to inconvenience you for a second night in a row, I gratefully accept." She turned to lever open the passenger door, unwilling to wait for him.

"Abby, wait—"

She charged into the house to start her day, knowing Vaughn was due at the hospital soon. She had a lot of supplies to gather. Materials he would arrange to transport for her. He remained charming and accommodating. A tender lover and a thoughtful friend.

He was on track to do everything right in making her heart yearn for him. Right up until the moment when he pulled away because he wasn't ready for a relationship.

Especially not a whole family.

She knew all of those things. Had understood them going into last night. It wasn't fair to take her disappointment out on Vaughn, when it was her own fault for letting her guard down around him.

But that didn't stop a whole lot of hurt from flooding through her as she changed her clothes and prepared for a day on the job site. Today, she was focusing on her art.

Her tribute to Alannah.

Any feelings for the sexy doctor were strictly off-limits.

* * *

Running a fishtail blade in a long sweep down the tree sculpture, Abigail watched the thin layer of wood peel away as she formed the smooth surface into carved bark.

She'd been crafting the sculpture for nearly twelve hours straight, stopping only to eat a quick bite in the hospital cafeteria a couple of times. And, of course, she'd had to stop to direct Micah's younger brother, Brandon, when he'd arrived with the additional limbs Abigail had requested.

He had been quicker and more efficient than the movers the day before and he'd refused her attempts to tip him, wheedling that what he really wanted was to work as her apprentice for the day and learn a new woodworking skill. She'd had reservations, certain Vaughn had planted that idea in his head. But Brandon had proven a quick and eager study, paying close attention to her demonstration for carving the joints to graft new pieces onto the tree. He'd had an occasional question or observation based on the kinds of wood she was using, impressing her with how fast he understood that various grains had different responses to the chisels and gouges she used.

His help had been invaluable, freeing her up to do the detail work she really wanted to complete before the hospital's summer gala. Not that she'd ever fully succeeded in chasing Vaughn from her thoughts today. She'd heard him paged earlier and had wondered what had happened.

If she was distracted from her work, she could always go back and fix mistakes, but a trauma surgeon didn't have that luxury. He had to be focused all the time or the difference could be a matter of life and death. The thought made her wish she'd tabled this morning's discussion until a later time.

Straightening from her efforts on the bark, she stepped back to view the texture of the piece.

A little girl in a hospital gown paused beside the caution tape surrounding the workspace. No more than seven or eight years old, the patient held hands with a nurse, trailing an IV cart as she pointed to the trunk.

"Are you carving a tree out of a tree?" she called over to Abigail. The auburn-haired sprite scrunched her nose as she looked at the sculpture, clearly perplexed.

"I am." Abigail stepped closer to her, setting aside the fishtail knife. "I'm starting with one big tree in the center, but I hope to add other trees all around it so you will feel like you're walking through a forest."

The child widened her green eyes and peered up at her nurse. "Wow. So even when it rains, it will be like we can go outside."

The nurse, a tall, willowy blonde in bright purple scrubs, explained, "Zoe is disappointed it's raining today. She likes it when we can go outdoors."

Abigail's chest squeezed in empathy, and she wondered how much time Zoe spent in the children's ward. Her admiration for Vaughn, and every other medical professional at Royal Memorial, notched higher. What a powerful gift to be able to improve someone's health and their quality of life.

"I'm going to hide surprises in the trees so you can spot something new each time you walk through."

Zoe lowered her voice to a stage whisper. "Like fairies?"

Abigail added one fairy to her to-do list.

"Maybe. You'll have to look very hard, though. Fairies are the best at hiding." Abigail wondered if her own child would be as bright-eyed and curious about the world.

Zoe did a happy dance that was sort of like running in place, until her nurse gently touched her head.

"We'd better let the artist return to her work," the nurse suggested, winking at Abigail over the girl's head. "Come on, sweetie."

The two of them strode off down the hall. In the corridor beyond the lounge, Abigail could see another young patient in her bathrobe and slippers, ready for bed.

Night had fallen without any sign of Vaughn since they'd parted ways this morning—him for the OR and a scheduled surgery, her for the children's ward.

She'd been hurt at the time, feeling shunned because of his retreat after their night together.

Yet she'd known even then that her reaction wasn't fair. She had put unrealistic expectations on him when he'd tried to make her aware that he had limitations when it came to connecting emotionally. She'd pushed for more, ready to move on from the disastrous night with her baby's father. But that didn't mean Vaughn had necessarily been ready for what had happened.

"Miss Abigail, are you done for the night?" Brandon called over to her, setting aside the buffer he'd been using to smooth out a rough patch in a peg.

The young man was twenty-four years old. The age her sister would never get to be. His revelation of his age—and the fact that his birthday had been just a few days ago—had been part of the reason Abigail couldn't send him away when he'd offered help. There had been something bittersweet about playing big sister, teaching him something and sharing her craft. But she was glad she'd done it.

"I am." She nodded, knowing she needed to go home and sleep. Put her feet up and take care of her body for her baby. "You've been an incredible help today."

Another gift from Vaughn that he'd shared even though she hadn't been particularly gracious. She promised herself to make it up to him. To do something nice to apologize. Over lunch today, she had finished her sketch of him—the one he'd caught her drawing that first day. She could make a present of that, maybe. They might not be lovers again, but perhaps they could salvage a friendship.

It surprised her how much that idea left her feeling hollow inside.

"Would you like me to come back tomorrow?" Brandon asked her as he straightened all the tools he'd been using, wrapping cords around the handles of small machines, brushing off the sawdust in his hand and tossing it in a waste can.

"I'm sure you have work you should be doing with your brother." She didn't want to take him away from his other duties, and she didn't feel right asking him to work more hours if he didn't allow her to pay him.

"I'll split my time then. Half a day here, half a day there." He laid a hand on the bark she'd carved. "I like working on something that will be in the hospital permanently."

How could she argue with that? She thought it was one of the coolest rewards of her job, too.

"In that case, I will be grateful for whatever help you want to give."

"Can I carry anything out for you? Help you to your car?" Brandon used a rag to wipe off the last blade she'd used before wrapping it on the leather case where she kept them.

"I'll be fine." She wanted to see if Vaughn was

still in the hospital. Try to make amends for coming down on him this morning. "But thank you."

Brandon scratched a hand under his ball cap, looking uncomfortable. "Doc C told me to make sure you didn't walk out to the parking lot alone."

Which made good sense. She was so tired she wasn't thinking straight. But before she could offer an alternative—like having Security walk her out later—a familiar voice sounded from behind her.

"That won't be necessary, Brandon." Vaughn stood on the other side of the caution tape, his green eyes locked on her. "I'll make sure Abigail gets home safely."

Eight

Eyes gritty from the worst day he'd had on the job since returning to Royal, Vaughn followed Abigail's car into downtown, making sure she arrived home without incident. She'd tried to wave off his insistence to accompany her into the house the first time she used the new alarm system, but in the end, she'd conceded. He had the feeling she'd only agreed out of concern for the safety of her baby, and not out of any romantic notions about him.

Which was fine. He didn't deserve for a woman like her to think about him that way when he couldn't even close his eyes to fall asleep while they shared a bed. But still, after the day he'd had, the knowledge that he'd hurt her added salt to the wounds he felt hours after he'd failed to save a gunshot victim.

In light of all that had gone wrong today, maybe it had been a mistake to stop by Abigail's work site to see her, let alone follow her home. But after hearing those heart monitors go flat on his nineteen-year-old patient, making sure Abigail was safe had become a priority that somehow carried him through the rest of a gut-shredding shift.

Ahead of him, Abigail's brake lights brightened. She parked in front of the bungalow as he pulled in the driveway behind her. He would simply walk her to the door, follow the instructions from the security company and make sure she knew how to arm the new system again before he left.

One step at a time. He would find a way to get through this day.

Preferably before the flashbacks started bombarding him, reminding him of other gunshots. Other victims. Other young men he had been powerless to heal.

He closed and locked the door behind him before moving toward Abigail's car to help her from the vehicle.

"Thank you." Stepping from the car, she smiled up at him as she took his hand. "You really didn't have to do this. Brandon talked me through how to use the new alarm today."

Vaughn couldn't articulate how much he needed to see with his own eyes that she was safe for the night, so he didn't try. "Brandon and his brother installed the same system at my house last year," he explained, walking her past the phlox, daisies and Texas bluebells she had planted on either side of the walkway.

Her skirt had blooms all over it, too, embroidered sunflowers on a blue background. The hem brushed the encroaching leaves of her runaway garden. She was a vibrant woman in every way, her lush curves making him ache to touch her. Hold her. As she reached the new security panel blinking dimly beside the front door, she turned to him. Waited while he checked his phone for the temporary code she was supposed to reset within forty-eight hours.

With a soft beep, the alarm was disarmed, allowing her to open the door.

"But explaining the alarm system was only a small way he helped me today. He has a gift for woodworking." She raked a hand through her dark hair, sifting curls behind one shoulder as she set her handbag on a table near the door and flicked on light switches that illuminated the kitchen and living area. She drew a deep breath, and her voice took on a different tone when she continued. "He is certainly very sharp and mature for someone who just turned twenty-four."

If Vaughn had forgotten her sister's age, he would have known it by the way Abigail carefully enunciated the number. *She would have been twenty-four*, she'd told him.

And by the way her eyes clouded over with still-fresh grief.

He didn't have much comfort to offer tonight, but he reached to pull her against him. Hell, maybe he did it for his own sake as much as hers. Because having her cheek rest on his chest, the scent of her hair in his nose, managed to steady him as they stood in the soft spotlight from a modern chandelier. He felt a breath shudder from her and guessed she felt the same thing as him.

A momentary ease. Shared strength. Connection.

And yes, undeniable attraction. Desire for her roared through him.

"I'm sorry about this morning," she told him, pulling back to peer up at him.

He frowned, not following. "You have nothing to apologize for."

She slid out of his arms and into the kitchen, pulling two bottles of water out of the small refrigerator and setting them on the breakfast bar.

"I was stressed about the police interview and the possibility of future talks with the FBI." She waved him toward one of the bar stools and then sat down in the other one at the counter. The bright red chair covers and chrome legs looked like the furnishings in a fifties' diner. "I snapped at you about buying the security system because you didn't want me at your place overnight." She sipped from her bottle, then pressed the cold plastic side of it to her forehead. "That was uncalled for."

He slid into the seat beside her, telling himself he'd only stay for another minute. Just long enough to clear up whatever it was she was feeling badly about since she hadn't done a damn thing wrong.

"I have a hard time sleeping at night," he admitted. Haltingly. Because he definitely didn't want to linger on the subject. "If you were getting the vibe that I was retreating, it was because I didn't want to fall asleep next to you and potentially..." Shout and freak her out? Lash out physically while he fought phantom combatants? "Wake you. If I had bad dreams."

Better that he sounded like a five-year-old battling a bogeymen than admit the truth. That his nightmares were flat-out terrifying for him and for anyone unfortunate enough to witness the event. Tonight, after losing a patient, he knew his brain would replay the worst of the worst.

He tipped some water to his dry lips, thinking he should forget about smoothing things over and just get out of her house now. Settle in for a rough night at home with his dog.

"Isn't that something Ruby helps with?" Her dark eyes were compassionate, but—thankfully—held no trace of pity.

Of course, she didn't know how bad it could get.

"Definitely. But I wasn't ready to trust the system with you there." He kept his explanation light on details and hoped it sufficed. Jittery from keeping his emotions in check all day, he speared to his feet, ready to leave. "I'd better let you get some sleep."

"Oh." She stood, too, setting down her water bottle. "I have something for you first."

Slipping past him, she disappeared into the shadows of her studio, where she hadn't turned on any lights. She returned with a thin leather portfolio and passed it to him.

"For me?" he asked, not sure what she'd be giving to him.

"It's just a little something. A gift to make up for the way things unfolded this morning."

"You didn't have to—" he began. Then, he saw the present.

His completed portrait rested inside. The same charcoal drawing he'd glimpsed in her papers that first day he'd come to her house.

The strokes of her pencil were sure and strong, the outline of his face captured indelibly. His hair. His shoulders.

Yet there was something else captured in the drawing. Something beyond his likeness. He saw a weariness in his face. A haunted look in the eyes. Was that how she saw him?

Or was that the reality of how he looked now? A changed man. Inexpressibly older than when he'd left Royal to be a brigade surgeon in Afghanistan.

"Vaughn?" Abigail gently covered her hand with his.

But he still couldn't speak. How could a beautiful young woman—a soon-to-be mother with a wealth of responsibilities on her shoulders—want to go anywhere near him?

Yet there she stood. With unmistakable longing in her eyes.

Tonight, he didn't stand a chance in hell of walking away.

Abigail wasn't sure how the image touched a nerve. But she could see that it had.

Vaughn was different tonight even before she'd shared the drawing with him. Remote. Polite but withdrawn.

Showing him the sketch had allowed her to glimpse behind that aloof mask, however. To darker emotions she knew he wanted to keep hidden. The moment happened so fast, she wondered if she'd seen it at all.

"Is everything okay?" she asked again. "I know art is highly subjective. And I only did a quick likeness, so I understand if it's not—"

"It's perfect. I mean—" He set aside the folder with the picture aside, laying it on the breakfast bar. "It is special to me because you made it."

She didn't want to push the issue. Her ego as an artist wasn't bruised since she knew the value of her work. But it was difficult not to ask a follow-up question when she simply wanted to understand this man better. Know what made him tick.

And yes, what made him pull away so hard.

"I'm glad you like it," she said finally, even though it came out too brightly. "And I didn't mean to keep you when you've had a long day."

He stared at her with an inscrutable look in his eyes. His whole body shifted, restlessly, even though his feet didn't move toward the door.

"I lost a patient this afternoon, Abby."

The words dropped into the room like a stone in a lake. Sinking. Sending ripples through the air that she could feel long after the sound faded.

If the mere idea of it made her ache with empathy, she couldn't imagine how he endured the pain of it.

"I'm so sorry." She clutched his hand, needing him to feel her presence. Her caring. For whatever that was worth. "It never occurred to me. I knew something was off—"

"I don't like to share it." He shook his head like he could deny her that empathy. "It's not your burden to bear. I picked this path. The good and the..."

He didn't finish the sentence. His eyes closed slowly.

"You chose a career that's a noble calling. A selfless one." She couldn't imagine doing his job. Choosing to wade into critical situations armed with education and experience, but knowing that wasn't always enough. "Most people couldn't carry the weight of life or death on their shoulders, but we're grateful to those who try."

She stepped closer to him, spanning his shoulders with her hands. Lightly squeezing her certainty into him as she flexed her fingers.

"The kid has been in the OR before." Vaughn's voice rasped drily. "One of my first major surgeries after I returned to Royal. He'd been shot then, too."

Abigail pressed her cheek against his chest as they stood together.

"You gave him a second chance then. He was fortunate that time."

"Afterward, he joked about it. Said he was getting out of his town while his luck held out. Moving somewhere else. Starting over." Vaughn's chin rested on her head, some small tension seeping away enough for him to relax into her. "He seemed like a decent kid."

"I'm sorry." She wrapped her arms around his waist. Breathing him in.

For a long moment, they stood together in her quiet kitchen with only the sound of Vaughn's heartbeat in her ear. Behind her, the clock ticked. Her refrigerator hummed.

Slowly, she edged away enough to glance up at him again. Their gazes locked. And something shifted between them. A tangible flicker of heat licked over her as the look in Vaughn's eyes changed.

She tried to ignore it since she was offering compassion, not indulging in the chemistry between them.

"Abby." He breathed her name like it was something precious. Something necessary. He focused on her as if he was seeing her for the first time all evening, his eyes turning a shade darker.

His hands gripped her hips. Fingers flexing.

She might have been able to deny her own need, but not his. Not tonight.

She slid her hands to the soft cotton that strained against his torso and let herself feel the tense heat of him. The strength.

He kissed her and she felt the sudden tide of physical desire roll over her like a rogue wave. It all but took out her knees, sending her swaying into Vaughn's arms so he could steady her. Hold her. Answer the plea for more with a demand of his own.

His tongue stroked hers, seeking, urging. She wrapped both arms around his neck, sealing her body to his, wanting the feel of his solid warmth against her.

Her sensitive, aching breasts molded to all that male strength and heat, sending a shiver through her. He lifted her, settling her on the kitchen table so he could step between her legs. A soft moan escaped her lips, a needy sound he sipped from her mouth with another kiss as he placed one hand on the small of her back to draw her hips closer to his.

His free hand traced the column of her throat,

sending more sensations racing up her spine. Her skin tightened, tingling, wanting his touch all over her. When his fingers dipped lower, beneath the neckline of her scoop-neck T-shirt, he slipped a hand beneath one lace cup of her bra, palming her breast. Plucking one taught nipple between his thumb and forefinger in a way that sent liquid heat flooding through her.

Desire sharpened. Pushing her higher.

Her world was spinning and she felt dizzy with want. He stripped off her shirt and it wasn't enough. She rolled her shoulders, shrugging off the straps of confining lace on her bra. Anything to be naked sooner. Faster.

So when Vaughn lowered a kiss to fasten around the other taut peak, the sensual swirl of his tongue threatened to make her fly right over the edge.

Need stormed over him.

Hot. Wild. Demanding.

Vaughn couldn't get enough of Abigail. Not her sweet mouth that he could kiss for days, or her beautiful body that tempted him beyond reason. It didn't matter what drove them together. Only this red-hot blaze of need that burned away everything else. All the reasons they shouldn't be together. All the reasons he wouldn't be right for her tomorrow.

Tonight, there was so much heat, so much hunger,

that nothing mattered but the next exquisite touch. The next mind-blowing kiss.

And that she was his.

He wanted her skin against his, her breathy moans in his ear, her legs wrapped around his hips. With impatient hands, he hauled up her skirt, sliding her to the edge of the table so the cradle of thighs met the hard thrust of his need. She felt so good. So right. For a moment, he had to close his eyes against the rising tide of want, fighting for control.

Her breathing was ragged, her hands restless on his shoulders, her nails skimming lightly up his back. He lifted her up, carrying her to a couch in the living room, wanting to be careful with her.

Protective of her beautiful body, he laid her down on the sofa in the far corner.

"Please," she whispered in his ear. "Don't stop."

He met her gaze, bright with desire. He wanted her more than he'd ever wanted a woman. Needed her beyond reason. He worked the buttons of his shirt with ruthless efficiency, shedding the button-down. His every thought of Abigail. Touching her. Tasting her. Filling her.

Making her his.

His belt was next, and his pants, though he had enough forethought to find the lone condom in his wallet. Set it aside.

All the while Abigail's gaze tracked him, her luscious breasts spilling out of the lace cups that his kisses had displaced. When he was naked, he returned to her, flicking open the clasp that held the bra in place. Freeing her to his touch.

His kiss.

She combed her fingers through his hair, arching her back to give him more access. Her skin was impossibly soft everywhere he touched. He raked down the zipper on her skirt, tugging the cotton lower until only a thin scrap of lace kept him from where he most wanted to be.

Seated beside her on the sofa where she was sprawled, he touched the damp lace. Skimmed it aside. Watched her cheeks flush with color, her head thrown back. Her heat flooded through to his fingers until he couldn't resist kissing her there. Licking her again and again until his name was a hoarse shout as she came for him.

Over and over.

Only then did he skim off the lace panties and settle between her legs. He rolled on the condom, his heart slamming inside his chest. By the time he slid inside her, inch by tantalizing inch, she wrapped her legs around him. Her arms. Kissed him with a passion he could taste.

The fire that raged inside him flared hotter. Searing over him. She met him, thrust for thrust, as lost in the moment as him. Each time her breath hitched, her lip caught between her teeth, it drove him higher. He wanted to feel her pleasure—that vibrant glow of her—all around him. It was the only thing that kept him in check when his body demanded release.

He rolled her on top of him, careful of the small curve of her belly. He let her set the pace at first, watching her face while her eyelids fluttered once. Twice.

Reaching between them, he stroked the tight bud of her sex.

Felt the answering shudder that went through her. He sat up just enough to palm one generous breast, guiding her to his mouth so he could kiss her there.

She cried out softly, her body sweetly responsive. He drove into her deeper. Harder. Her fingers fisted in his hair, her lips parted on a silent cry.

And then he felt her release shudder through her, raining sweetness all around him until his own restraint fell away. Pleasure overran him. Inundated him. He couldn't do a damn thing but hold on to Abigail, steadying them both as sensation bombarded them. This time when she called out his name, he shouted hers in an echo of bliss. Total fulfillment.

A devastating oneness than robbed him of breath and left him panting for long moments afterward.

He'd never felt such utter contentment in the silence that followed. His breathing slowed as she fell on top of him, her beautiful body curling into his as naturally as if they'd slept together for a lifetime.

Tugging a lightweight blanket off the back of the

sofa, he pulled it around her and kissed the top of her dark hair.

He caressed her shoulder through the veil of curls that fell around her. Breathed in the spicyandcitrus scent of her fragrance.

And wondered how he'd ever walk away.

Nine

Abigail wouldn't allow herself to fall asleep.

Not when she knew how stressed Vaughn had been the last time they had shared a bed together, spending too long wondering if he would have nightmares and how to avoid waking her up. She regretted that he experienced that kind of anxiety, but she empathized even though she couldn't possibly fully understand what he was going through. But she'd seen the agony in his eyes. She couldn't bear for him to go through that again.

So after he'd stroked her hair and kissed her temple for a while, she sat up. Reaching for his shirt, she slid her arms into the fabric that held his scent.

"Aren't you exhausted?" he asked, levering up on his elbow. "Was I keeping you awake?"

"I thought I'd make something to eat before you have to go home." She said it matter-of-factly, like it was no problem that they couldn't share a bed for sleeping. After her brief fling with a man who had deceived all of Royal, Abigail was willing to compromise to be with a man of Vaughn's integrity. "Would you like some chicken? I made a big batch of it on the weekend so I'd have leftovers."

Ten minutes later, they juggled plates of cold fried chicken, raw veggies and hummus and made themselves comfortable on her love seat. Hardly an exotic feast, but it all tasted good after the hospital cafeteria food she'd eaten on the run today while working. Or at least, she thought it tasted good. Perhaps he was used to richer fare.

"This is the best fried chicken I've ever eaten." Vaughn dug into a second piece. He'd dressed again, minus his shirt, since she was wearing it.

It was a good trade in her eyes, since now she had the added benefit of sitting across from a shirtless, sexy doc.

He seemed more relaxed now. His emotions more under control. For that, she was grateful. She hoped it meant he would be able to sleep soundly tonight.

"Thank you. I avoid fried foods for the most part." She swirled a carrot through hummus. "But I draw the line at chicken. This is my grandmother's recipe and my ultimate comfort food."

"This is open-a-restaurant good." He set down

a bone and wiped his fingers on the napkins she'd brought out.

His obvious enjoyment pleased her, making her think of happier times with her family. "My grandmother was born and bred in southern Louisiana, but she moved to Texas when my granddaddy swept her off her feet. She taught Alannah and me all her Cajun recipes. But the chicken was always my favorite."

"Cajun?" He sipped the sweet tea she'd poured for them.

"I dial back the pepper in my version," she admitted. "But my grandmother's original recipe was definitely more Cajun than Southern."

"So with all those culinary skills at your fingertips, what made you decide to be an artist?"

"It wasn't a decision, per se." She'd always found it difficult to explain her path in a way that made sense to people. "I feel like I was born an artist. Making things has always been natural to me. When I would go out into the world—on a hike with my sister and to the grocery store with my mother—I would draw a picture of it when I got home."

Vaughn grinned as he reached for another serving. "I guess I did that, too, when I was a kid."

"The difference is, I never stopped. I never got tired of sharing what I saw and how I felt about it." Standing, she picked up one of her sketchbooks from the closest table in her studio and brought it back to the coffee table in front of the love seat. "Even now, if you look through my drawings, they're mostly everyday things. I express myself through my pictures. They're like a journal of what I experience."

Flipping through the pages, she saw the past months flash before her. Images of Royal. Of nature out her window. Of the tiny human being growing inside her.

"Wow." Vaughn set aside his plate and wiped his fingers on a napkin to study the images with her. He pointed to the ultrasound picture, a rough interpretation of her last time there. "That's amazing."

The awe in his voice reminded her how monumentally her life was about to change.

"Isn't it? I'm going back next week for another ultrasound since the baby didn't cooperate for a gender reveal at the twenty-week appointment." She couldn't wait.

But at the same time, it was one of those big moments in the pregnancy that she wished she could have shared with a supportive, excited partner.

Instead, she would be there alone.

"When did you realize you could take the art you make every day and turn it into a career?" He set aside her sketches to finish his meal.

"In college. I pursued art because that's what made me happy. My teachers were supportive and helped me to find outlets at local galleries. I was selling small works even then."

"Because you're incredibly talented," he said without hesitation.

She knew the value of her work, yet still, his compliment made her cheeks heat. "I'm not sure if it's talent so much as my perspective." She'd thought long and hard about that. "I think people like seeing the world through my eyes."

She'd wondered if she would lose that connection when her sister died. If her perspective would become too dark. Too depressing. But she didn't worry about that now. Her art was a reflection of her, no matter what she experienced. She couldn't change that or she would risk alienating her muse.

Vaughn studied her thoughtfully.

"What made you move from drawing to sculpture?"

"A visit to Galveston with my sister. We went exploring on the beach and found some driftwood." That vacation had been so happy. Alannah had been seventeen and Abigail had just turned twenty-two. She'd felt so grown-up taking her sister on a weekend trip to the beach. "I wanted to make something with it when I got home. I discovered I loved working with wood."

She set aside her plate, trying not to get lost in the past as the happy part of the memory faded, bringing with it the darker side. Clearing her throat of the swell of sudden emotions, she continued.

"We used to say that trip was a turning point for both of us. I found the joy of sculpture and she realized a new passion for kayaking." The words hurt her throat as the memory weighted down her heart. "We went together, that first time. She thought it was the best thing, being out on the water with no motor. Just the quiet splash of water off the paddle."

Vaughn set aside his dishes to move closer. Sliding an arm around her shoulders, he pulled her near.

"I'm sorry." He kissed the top of her head. Squeezed her upper arm lightly. "It wasn't fair to lose her so young."

"She was training to work as a firefighter." Her sister had been fearless. "I was so worried about her being the one to run into burning buildings, never thinking she might get hurt doing something recreational. Something that should have been safe."

Tears leaked from her eyes, making her realize how deeply she'd wandered into the past when she hadn't intended to. Vaughn stroked her hair like he could have comforted her all night, but that wasn't fair to him.

She levered herself to sit upright. "I'm sorry. I meant to feed you and let you get back home before it got any later."

"I'm glad to learn more about you." His green eyes followed her as she started scooping up the dishes. "Let me get those."

He plucked them out of her hands.

"I'll go change so you can have your shirt back." She was scavenging for excuses to leave the room, needing to rein in her runaway emotions.

The last time she'd shared her grief with a man,

it had all but overwhelmed her. And while she trusted Vaughn not to take advantage of her feelings, she didn't trust herself to maintain control of her boundaries.

Those boundaries were the only way her heart was going to survive this relationship with a man who became more important to her every day.

The hospital summer gala was more than a reception to unveil Abigail's statue, although for Vaughn, that was the most exciting part.

Vaughn had a role to play glad-handing donors to the hospital's trauma center, as well as those who supported the new art installation in the children's ward. He'd visited the barber earlier in the day for a trim, letting the guy shave off his beard while he was at it.

He looked like an entirely different man. More like the military officer he'd been throughout his deployment. He'd been keeping that side of himself at bay, trying to bury his memories, but that hadn't worked.

As he dressed in the requisite monkey suit for the event, he adjusted the bow tie he couldn't get quite right and wondered what Abigail would see when she looked at him tonight. The same world-weary man she'd started sketching that first day they'd met? Or was there more life in his eyes these days, now that she had come into his world with her vibrant outlook?

Vaughn didn't know. He couldn't tell what he saw when he looked in the mirror anyhow. From behind him on the bed, Ruby lifted her head to study him. Apparently she didn't see anything too far off base since she settled her head back on her paws and let her eyes drift closed again.

He was pretty sure the dog missed Abigail.

After that night Abby had spent at his house, Ruby went into the spare room where she'd slept a few times. She'd circled the bed. Nosed the drawer where she'd helped unpack Abigail's few things. Then she'd padded back out into the hall to lie by the door.

Not often. But she'd never done that before Abigail's appearance in their lives.

"Maybe we'll see her again tonight if I'm lucky," he told Ruby, scratching behind her ears.

Since the night when he'd let his guard down at her place, confiding his loss of the patient, he'd been at work two of the three days. He'd finished off those two shifts by visiting her at the children's ward, both times finding Brandon working beside her. Lifting tree limbs into place at her direction, and fastening them onto joints he'd made himself.

Vaughn planned to make a sizable donation to the guy's business start-up fund, although both times he'd mentioned it, Brandon had waved off the suggestion with an assurance that he was learning a lot. That made Vaughn happy even as he wondered what Abigail would have done on her own. Would she have lifted those limbs over her head to extend the size of that tree?

He scowled just thinking about it, but he hadn't wanted to ask her when she was hard at work. She'd texted him last night—on his off day—to show him a photo of her smiling in front of the completed tree. Vaughn had been touched that she'd thought of him, but worried what it meant for them that her primary project at the hospital was finished.

Would he see her after tonight? Sure, her work would continue at the children's ward, but not at this pace. And much of it would be accomplished in her studio and brought to the hospital at a later date. So the days of seeing her regularly were over. The realization nagged at him, pushing him to think of other ways to keep her in his life.

Which made no sense because he'd known from the start that the relationship couldn't really go anywhere. He didn't want a family and she needed to think about her future with her child.

His cell phone chimed before he could leave for the gala, alerting him to a call from a private number. He debated not answering but he was ahead of schedule.

"Chambers," he answered, peering out the back window onto the lawn overlooking the woods where he'd walked with Abigail that day.

"Vaughn, it's Will Sanders."

Just hearing the name sent a weird reaction tumbling through his gut. Abigail had been with a man she believed to be Will the night her child had been conceived. She still thought of that man as "Will." So the surge of jealousy Vaughn experienced at hearing the name was obviously misplaced.

And, considering the hell this guy had been through, would be a slap in the face if he knew.

"It's good to hear from you, Will." Vaughn pulled the blinds on the view and double-checked the lock on the sliding glass doors. Ruby appeared in the room behind him, no doubt remembering it was suppertime.

"I wanted to let you know that I'm putting my personal resources into the investigation of the imposter situation."

"Can't blame you there. Any man would want justice." Vaughn filled Ruby's water and food dishes.

Micah would take the dog out for a walk soon.

"I've hired a detective, Cole Sullivan, from a local private security firm to find Jason Phillips."

"He's with the Walsh Group." Vaughn knew the firm and the man since Cole was a member of the Texas Cattleman's Club. "My father considered hiring him when the oil company executives received some death threats last year."

Cole was a former Texas Ranger and as sharp as they came. But then Vaughn's father had decided to increase his home security system and hand over the threats to the police instead.

"If anyone can get to the bottom of this, I trust Cole to be the man." Will sounded grim. Resolute.

"But the first person he wants to talk to is Abigail Stewart, since she may be the last person to have seen him alive besides Rich."

A chill raced up Vaughn's spine.

The thought of Abby being mixed up with guys like that scared the hell out of him. And made him more determined than ever to stick close to her until they figured out where Rich and Jason had disappeared.

"Tonight Abigail will be at the hospital gala with me, unveiling her new statue for the children's ward." He wanted to suggest another day to interview her since Vaughn wanted tonight to be special for her. She deserved the time to enjoy having the spotlight on her work.

"Cole already knows and plans to be there. I'm only calling to give you a heads-up since I got the impression the two of you are close."

Hell. He was more transparent than he knew when it came to Abigail.

"I appreciate that." Vaughn grabbed his keys, in a new hurry to get to the gala. He didn't want Abigail to face another round of questions alone. "Cole is a good guy but he can be…intimidating to those who don't know him."

Will gave a dry laugh. "Let's hope so. I need him to cut through the red tape and figure out where that bastard Rich went. I feel certain that Jason isn't to blame for any of this, but then again, who knows." He sounded frustrated. Angry. "We need to locate him."

"Thanks for the call, Will."

"I figured you'd want to be with her," he said simply before disconnecting.

As Vaughn slid into the driver's seat of the Mercedes coup he liked to use for work, he wondered how Will Sanders had deduced the truth that he had battled for over a week to deny.

He might have every reason in the world not to pursue this relationship with Abigail. But the plain truth of the matter was, he wanted to be with her. And he didn't see that changing anytime soon.

Scanning Royal Memorial's rooftop garden for any sign of Vaughn, Abigail declined a second offer of champagne from a passing waiter. Since the summer gala was a fund-raiser in addition to an unveiling for her statue, the event planner had spared no expense to make it elegant. Abigail had nearly fallen over when she heard what the tickets to the event cost, but then, the function raised money for much-needed hospital equipment and programs.

White lights had been strung from the trees, creating a fairy canopy overhead. Chamber musicians played for the cocktail hour, which was currently in progress, but she'd heard a popular country band would take the stage afterward to kick off the dancing. Tall sunflowers swayed in the breeze from discreetly placed fans to keep the place cool while the sun set. Even the sky had cooperated for the gala, turning the clouds bright pink and purple.

She longed for her sketchbook and a place to draw, needing to capture this beautiful night in her memory. The unveiling of the statue was a moment that belonged to Alannah as much as Abigail, since she'd dedicated the project to her sister's love of nature. Alannah would love the "Secret Garden" theme of the party, with white tapers flickering in the breeze on a display table of cut flowers that labeled all the blooms taken from the surrounding garden. The floral arrangements ranged from natural wildflower bouquets to more exotic and artful groupings.

The scent of jasmine hung heavy in the air, the profuse blooms lining the railings around the rooftop. The greeters at the door downstairs had given all the women gardenia blooms to wear as wrist corsages, another fragrant note so rich and decadent Abigail wanted to fill her studio with them. Although, not as much as she wanted to see Vaughn tonight.

She plucked a glass of sparkling water with lemon from a tray near the bar, grateful for the nonalcoholic drink options in easy reach. Sipping from the commemorative glass with an etched rose, she scanned the sea of tuxedos while discreetly tugging at her dress hem. She hadn't expected the addition of a baby bump to make finding clothing so awkward. The burgundy-colored dress she'd borrowed from an online rental store was appropriately elegant and a designer she'd never be able to afford outright. But the swell of baby made the dress ride up her hips, where it was snug. Thankfully, a layer of tulle over the sleek satin sheathe still kept her figure a mystery. The dress made the most of her legs and the more curvy breasts that came with pregnancy.

"Abigail Stewart?" One of the tuxedo-wearing guests stepped out of the line at the bar to stalk toward her.

Unfortunately, he was not the handsome doctor she sought.

This man had dark blond hair and piercing blue eyes, his strong shoulders and athletic build the kind of physique she'd seen on local ranchers. There was something about their gait, perhaps. The way they carried themselves.

"Yes?" She set aside her water glass to introduce herself, thinking the stranger might be someone interested in the statue. She'd already fielded a few questions about her work. "I'm Abigail."

"Cole Sullivan." He thrust his hand toward her, his blue eyes fixing on her. "I'm a private investigator retained by Will Sanders."

She stiffened at the name, even as she told herself the real Will Sanders was a perfectly nice man. A man who'd been cruelly impersonated and swindled by a former friend.

"Nice to meet you." She shook his hand, wondering how she could have misread a private eye for a rancher.

"I'd like to ask you a few questions if you have a minute?"

She hesitated, not wanting to ruin her big night with a bout of nerves.

"I'll be sure you don't miss your entrance for the statue unveiling," Cole assured her.

Anxiety fluttered through her. She really needed to help him. To protect her child's future, she was invested in finding Rich Lowell and holding him accountable for everything he'd done. But she regretted the timing for this interview during an important night for her career.

Before she could respond, Vaughn separated himself from the crowd, reaching her side with three long strides. A bolt of relief—and the ever-present desire—shot through her to see him. He looked incredible in his perfectly fitted tuxedo and—more surprisingly—a clean-shaven face that revealed a slight scar along the bottom of his chin that gave his handsome face character. And made her want to kiss him right there.

"You look beautiful, Abigail," he murmured, sliding a possessive arm around her waist and drawing her against his side. Then he turned his attention to the private investigator. "Cole Sullivan, it's been a long time." He shook the man's hand and the two men exchanged pleasantries.

Cole was a member of the Texas Cattleman's Club, apparently, and a local rancher who worked part-time for the Walsh Group. The former Texas Ranger handled the security firm's most challenging cases.

All of which she gleaned in the rapid back-and-forth between the men before Cole repeated his original request.

"I'd like to speak to Ms. Stewart for a few minutes, Vaughn." The PI's gaze returned to her. "I believe she was just about to agree to that."

Anxiety spiked again. No doubt about it, Cole Sullivan made her nervous. Or maybe it was simply the thought of revisiting that night at the Ace in the Hole and the fight she'd seen there. Knowing how close she might have come to real danger was scary.

"May I join you?" Vaughn turned toward her, the question directed toward her and not Cole.

Vaughn's green eyes searched hers, warming her insides and soothing some of the jitters she'd been feeling.

"I would appreciate that." She'd like his company, his touch, his presence in her life a whole lot more than he would ever know.

But for right now, she was just grateful she wouldn't be facing more questioning alone.

"Fair enough." Cole nodded his satisfaction with the plan. "Where can we speak privately? This isn't a conversation I want anyone else to overhear."

Ten

Vaughn glanced back at Abigail as they left the rooftop garden with Cole, descending the stairs that led toward his office, where they could speak privately.

She looked incredible. The mass of dark hair was gathered at the nape of her neck, the glossy curls spilling down the center of her back. Her scarlet-colored cocktail gown had a floaty fabric around it that gave her the look of an ethereal creature, like one of the winged fairies he'd seen her carve in hidden nooks in the sculpture she'd made.

More than that, she glowed. He'd heard that about pregnant women, but had never noticed it with his own eyes the way he could see it in Abigail. Her skin had the dewy appearance that women tried to recreate with makeup, her cheeks pink with good health. When Vaughn had first seen her at the party he'd done a double take. Not that she was more beautiful in extravagant clothing, because he thought she was perfect in the tennis shoes and T-shirts she favored for work. But seeing her tonight was like discovering a new side of her, another fascinating facet to a woman who intrigued him at every turn.

"Thank you for joining us." She said the words softly as he led her and Cole Sullivan out of the stairwell and into the corridor that led to his office. "I feel better having you here with me."

With Cole a few steps behind her, checking messages on his phone, she probably thought their conversation was private enough. Although Vaughn would lay money Cole didn't miss much.

"I'm hoping to wrangle a dance out of you in return." He wanted to spend every minute of this evening with her, in fact, although some of his evening would need to be devoted to mingling.

Securing donations.

Because while the cost of admission covered the expense of the party as well as some money toward necessary hospital improvements, Royal Memorial counted on this well-heeled segment of the community for more than that. Vaughn was reasonably good at securing those kinds of donations, too. He had sacrificed the easy path in life—taking over his father's business—to make a difference in the world. He walked the walk. So he didn't mind urging people with deep pockets to make a difference by writing a check.

"I'll definitely be ready for a dance afterward." Her eyes glowed with warmth. With awareness.

Vaughn was glad to have distracted her from the questioning for a minute at least. The stress of those worries wasn't good for her...or the baby. He opened the door to his office with a key card that tracked hours and time of use for the space. The medical arts building was attached to Royal Memorial, but occupied its own wing.

"Come on in." Vaughn flipped on the lights, then held the door for both of them before letting it fall shut behind them. Inside, there was a consultation area with a couch and two chairs, so he wasn't stuck sitting behind a desk when speaking to patients. The dynamic put people more at ease.

He took a seat beside Abigail on the low gray sofa, leaving Cole to take the chair opposite them. Abigail's eyes wandered around the space briefly before Cole asked her to recount the night she'd gone to Ace in the Hole. While she shared the story Vaughn already knew, he wondered what she'd seen when she looked around the office.

He'd always viewed it as functional. But seeing the couple of generic canvases that had come with the room, he wondered what she thought of his complete lack of personal investment in his surroundings.

He'd never really thought it before, always fully focused on his work when he walked through the door.

"Did you hear anything specific in the exchange?" Cole asked Abigail now. "Any snippets of conversation or shouted words?"

"There was name-calling and swearing." She shook her head. "I remember some of the more colorful expletives, but I couldn't tell you which voice said what. They were gasping for air, rolling around the floor. It distorted both their voices."

Cole looked up from the notes he was tapping into his phone. He'd asked permission to record the conversation, and he was doing so, but he'd been making notes the whole time, too.

"Could there have been a third voice in that room? Someone else in there that you didn't see?"

"Sure. Maybe." She shrugged, hesitating in a way that revealed her nervousness. "I couldn't see the whole room from where I peered in through a crack in the open door. But I didn't hear any extra set of feet scuffling or anything. And it seems like I would have heard a third person moving around to at least escape the mayhem of Jason and Rich throwing punches."

"Right. Maybe." Cole's forehead scrunched in concentration as he reviewed his screen. "And you're sure of the time and date?"

"Positive." Abigail chewed her lip for a moment. "I kept looking at the calendar that week, trying to tell myself I had plenty of time to tell him about the baby—"

Cole interrupted, "Rich Lowell is the father of your child?"

Vaughn wrapped an arm around her waist, wanting her to feel his presence. To take whatever comfort she could from him being by her side. He understood it couldn't be easy for her to focus on the joy of becoming a mother when the child's father could return to Royal at any time.

The thought sparked a sudden wish that Vaughn could claim her baby as his. Hell, he wished he could claim her, too.

Foolish, fanciful notions.

But she would be safer if both those things were true, damn it.

Abigail's hand shifted protectively to her baby bump. "If Rich Lowell was the man impersonating Will Sanders, then yes." Her voice shook and she drew a deep breath. "Rich Lowell is the father of this child."

"Rich was absolutely the imposter." Cole sat back in his chair, setting aside his phone. "I've stopped recording, by the way. And I appreciate you answering my questions."

A little of the tension in Abigail's body eased. Vaughn could feel it as she relaxed slightly.

"I'm glad I could help. Or rather, I hope I've helped."

Cole nodded. "You're the last person to see Jason besides Rich."

"Can you tell us your next move? What you're doing to push through this stalemate the law enforcement agencies seem to have reached in the investigation?" Vaughn hated not knowing where Rich was. The sooner the imposter was behind bars, the better.

"For starters, I'm going back to the urn that Jason Phillips sent to his sister along with the note she received about Will's death." Cole threaded his fingers together behind his head as he leaned back. "I need to get the contents of the urn retested in case there is DNA present in bone fragments."

"But you know it's not Rich, right?" Abigail asked, her fingers toying with the hem of her dress where it fell over her knee.

"Correct. What I'd like to do next is see if it matches anyone else."

"Jason." Vaughn supplied the obvious answer.

Abigail's hand sought his before she spoke.

"You don't think he killed Jason?" she asked, worry evident in her voice.

With good reason.

"He left Will for dead off Cabo San Lucas." Cole's voice was grim. "And he's spent more of Will's money than he could ever repay. So I'd call Rich Lowell a desperate man."

Vaughn shifted his hold on Abigail, moving his hand to her back to rub soothing circles along her shoulders. She shouldn't have to deal with any of this right now.

"Jason might have found out that Will was a fake and called him on it." Vaughn tried to envision what could have precipitated the brawl Abigail had witnessed.

"Or he could have uncovered missing money and alerted Will," Cole added. "But I'm also having the note that arrived with the urn reviewed by a handwriting expert to see if it's a match with Jason's writing."

Vaughn's finger rubbed along Abigail's back, strands of her hair clinging to his wrist. "Smart thinking."

"Will is committed to getting to the bottom of this mess. He's even flying in some tech genius from Silicon Valley who thinks he's got a software answer for all of this. Luke Weston from West-Tech." Cole shrugged. "And while that may or may not work, I can assure you we're putting every available resource on this."

"Good." Abigail seemed to have regained her composure. She straightened in her seat. "We'll rest easier once we know what happened."

"We'll find out." Cole's smile was predatory. Certain. "We'll locate Rich Lowell, too."

Vaughn noticed the investigator didn't promise the same for Will's right-hand man, Jason Phillips.

Still, the investigation was moving in the right direction. Progress being made. But that didn't mean Abigail and her child were safe. And until they were, Vaughn couldn't walk away.

He couldn't deny feeling relieved that he didn't have to yet. Guilt bit him hard, since he knew that him sticking around could lead to their feelings growing. Deepening.

Frustrated, he bolted out of his office once the interview was over. He would see Abigail at the party, of course. But first, he would throw himself into fund-raising and give them both a breather.

Half an hour later, Abigail followed Belinda McDowell, the Royal Memorial development officer, who'd led the meeting the day she was hired. The woman was in charge of the statue's unveiling. An announcement had been made at the rooftop party, inviting guests to join them for a brief ceremony in the children's ward since the sculpture was too huge to transport upstairs.

The whole party didn't relocate, of course, but Abigail was flattered to see how many of Royal's most prominent citizens had turned out to support the hospital and see her artwork. Her career had taken an exciting turn already with this commission and, with any luck, more gallery sales and special projects would follow. She'd told Vaughn that she'd been fortunate to do what she loved for work. But with a baby on the way, she might not always have that luxury. If she couldn't support herself and her child with her creativity, she would end up doing temp jobs again.

When they reached the children's ward lounge, Abigail could see temporary wall partitions had been rolled into place to protect the privacy of the ward and the patients from the unveiling ceremony. An arbor of flowers stood in front of the tree sculpture, which had been partially hidden with a gauzy black curtain. Of course, the statue was so huge the branches spilled out of the top, crawling along the high ceilings where Brandon had helped to secure them. Abigail had carved for hours to add the details she wanted on those high limbs, but she knew she would add more bark and hidden creatures to the hard-to-reach places throughout the coming year when she developed her idea for an interactive forest.

For now, however, the sculpture was impressive enough for the unveiling. Abigail peered behind her for a glimpse of Vaughn, certain he must have come downstairs with the rest of the attendees who'd chosen to see the statue. He'd been such a steadying presence during her questioning with Cole Sullivan.

She'd been anxious for that dance Vaughn had promised, but he'd been quick to melt into the crowd when they returned from the interview in his office. She knew that was part of his job tonight.

And yet…she wondered if he was also astutely distancing himself from her in front of his colleagues. By the people in the community he hoped would donate more funds to the hospital. Was her presence—an increasingly obvious *pregnant* presence—a detriment to his efforts? Some might view her pregnancy as being on the scandalous side. Especially Vaughn's fellow members of the Texas Cattleman's Club, who were privy to details surrounding Rich Lowell's misdeeds while impersonating Will. While Abigail wasn't the only woman Rich had used and mistreated, she felt like she played a larger role in her own deception than any of the other women. She'd knowingly had a fling with a married man.

She'd been too lost in her grief to question Rich's insistence that he and his wife, Megan Phillips-Sanders, were separated. Although she didn't feel the need to share her personal journey of mourning with the world, she also understood why some people would judge her harshly.

Her thoughts swirling, she almost bumped into the hospital development officer as she paused in front of the flower archway in the children's ward. The older woman wore a black strapless gown with a matching short-sleeve sequin jacket. The long column of simple lines suited her no-nonsense approach.

"Ms. Stewart, if you would stand right here—" she pointed to a spot beside the microphone "—I'll introduce you before the unveiling."

"Thank you." Excited to share her work with the group, Abigail's pleasure was dimmed only by the fact that she didn't see Vaughn yet.

"Do you wish to say a few words?" Belinda asked, testing the sound equipment.

"No. Thank you." She'd dedicated the project to Alannah in her mind. She didn't need to share that story with the group. Besides, she liked for her work to be interpreted individually, without swaying viewers to share her highly personal vision.

"Very well." Belinda took her place on a small platform. "I'm going to get started."

Abigail discreetly lifted up on her toes, trying to see through the crowd for Vaughn. She really thought he'd wanted to see this. To share this with her.

She'd come to rely on him so quickly even though they hadn't known each other long. Now that she would be spending less time at the hospital, would their relationship fade, too? She had an ultrasound appointment at the hospital on Monday—her last trip to Royal Memorial for a while and for a much different reason. She'd thought about asking him to join her.

But was that selfish of her when she knew he wasn't ready for more?

"Ladies and gentlemen, may I have your attention, please?" The hospital administrator took the microphone, quieting the assembled guests before briefly discussing the commitment of the hospital staff to excellence, right down to providing a nurturing environment for patients.

She introduced Abigail as the artist of the hospital's latest attempt to create an uplifting retreat for patients and their families. As the crowd clapped politely, she heard a soft but unmistakable whistle of approval from the back of the room. A few chuckles followed, along with people turning to spot the source of the whistling.

Those turned heads allowed her to spot Vaughn. For a moment, their eyes met and her heart turned a somersault.

He was here.

He lifted a hand in a wave of acknowledgment.

No matter that she was worried about how people would react to them together, apparently he had no such reservations.

"Without further ado," Belinda McDowell continued, "I present to you our very own *Tree of Gifts*."

The black gauzy curtain fell to the ground at her verbal cue, revealing the sculpture in spotlight.

There were appreciative oohs and aahs that sounded genuine to Abigail's hopeful ears. Even the applause that followed was deeper, louder and more prolonged than the earlier polite smattering. And if she'd had any doubt about the positive reception, Belinda McDowell's wide smile told her she saw the unveiling as a success.

Then, just as the clapping began to die down, Belinda returned to the microphone. "Before you leave, ladies and gentlemen, make sure to spot a few of the gifts inside the tree."

Behind her, the spotlight darted to one of the carved owls perched in an obvious nest on a low limb. Then to a more subtle face in the bark.

"You can tell us which one of these surprises you love best," Belinda continued. "And you can bid on the chance to have your name carved on your favorite."

Event volunteers began passing out white cards for guests to make bids on the small pieces of art in the tree, the surprises Abigail had installed for bored and restless children to find as they walked through the lounge. She had to hand it to resourceful event staff for making the most of the statue at the gala. It was a quick, easy way to earn more donations and give guests buy-in on the project.

Seeing her part in the unveiling finished, Abigail stepped away from the flower arch and out of the way of guests who were excited to find new creatures hidden in the limbs. She, on the other hand, was looking through the crowd for Vaughn.

She spotted him at last, speaking with a distinguished-looking older man and woman, still standing at the back of the room. She debated returning to the party upstairs, not wanting to interrupt him if he was speaking to friends or touting the merits of the hospital's mission to potential donors.

But before she could dart away for the stairs, he spotted her. Waved her over to join him.

"Abigail." His smile seemed strained. "I'd like you to meet my parents."

Eleven

Vaughn saw his mother's eyes zero in on Abigail's pregnant belly like a laser beam.

Her look made him belatedly realize this meeting was bound to be awkward. At the time he'd waved Abigail over, he'd been more concerned she would leave the event if she didn't see him. And, selfishly, he'd been grateful for an excuse to dodge his parents' questions about his mental health. They'd been hammering on about the importance of keeping Ruby close by whenever he wasn't working. Hell, they'd brought up switching to a less demanding job, suggesting he come back to the family business, where there would be less stress.

As if he would waste the skills and education he'd spent almost a lifetime acquiring.

Unfortunately, he'd probably made the leap from frying pan to fire. And chances were good he was taking Abigail with him into the hot seat. Her eyes darted toward him as she made her way over, her uncertainty quickly masked as she reached his side.

He had no choice now but to forge ahead.

"Mom, Dad, this is Abigail Stewart, the artist who created the *Tree of Gifts*." He wasn't sure how else to introduce her. He certainly hadn't thought to ask her ahead of time about their first public appearance together.

They weren't a couple. And yet…to say nothing about their relationship denied her importance to him.

"Hello." Abigail shook their hands, smiling warmly while Vaughn kicked himself. "It's so nice to meet you."

The moment had passed to clarify a relationship. He could see his parents' avid curiosity while they murmured polite greetings.

"Abigail, my parents, David and Bronwyn Chambers." Vaughn knew the burden was on him to extract Abigail from the conversation quickly and efficiently.

He'd never intended to spring a meet-the-parents moment on her tonight. Abigail's gaze flashed to his for a moment. Questioning.

"Your sculpture is beautiful, Abigail." His mother waved the white donation card that she held, along with a small pencil. "I was just going up to take a closer look so I could see what we should bid on. Perhaps you'd steer me toward one of your favorites?"

"Of course." Abigail stepped back, opening up a path toward the sculpture for his mother. "Let's go see."

Vaughn was ready to sprint into action right behind them, but his mother turned back with a steely look in her green eyes. "Gentleman, excuse us," she said firmly. "We'll be right back."

He wanted to concoct a reason to join them. But Abigail narrowed a look at him that he couldn't quite interpret. Was she hurt that he hadn't claimed a relationship with her? Aggravated? Either way, her expression warned him that she would handle his mother on her own.

He wasn't certain how he knew that. But he understood her silent message just the same. He must be starting to know Abigail very well that they could communicate so acutely that way. Still, he felt defeated as he watched his mother sail off toward the sculpture, her navy blue caftan billowing behind her.

What the hell would they be discussing?

"You walked right into that one," his father observed at his elbow. He clapped a hand on Vaughn's back.

"I disagree, Dad." He ground his teeth together. "I never saw it coming."

"Is the baby yours?" Dad asked. No judgment. Just a question.

Albeit a loaded one.

Vaughn hissed out a breath between his teeth, wondering if his mother was being just as tactful right now with Abigail.

"No." He lowered his voice, making sure they weren't overheard. "I would have mentioned it before now if I was going to be a father."

His dad's hand slid away from his shoulders. "There was a time I would have thought that, too. But we don't hear much from you these days."

Emotions piled on his chest, one after the other. Regret. Frustration. Worry for Abigail. Resentment that their time together was going to end and he wasn't any closer to figuring out how to be a fully functioning half of a couple anymore.

"I'm working on it, Dad," he said finally, not sure what else to say. "That's all I can do."

His gaze landed on Abigail—where she stood beside his mother. She was shaking her head. Emphatic denial. His mother was touching her shoulder. Reassuring her?

It was too much for him. He had to intervene in case his mother was making assumptions about their relationship. Or about Abigail herself. She certainly didn't owe anyone any explanations about her choices or her future. And there was a chance his mother was trying to wheedle both of those things from the woman he cared about.

He might not be the right man for Abigail, but if

she was still speaking to him by the time he arrived at her side, he was going to find a way to make it up to her.

"Honestly, Mrs. Stewart." Abigail was trying to make her point another way, hoping to reassure Bronwyn Chambers as they stood under the sprawling branches of the *Tree of Gifts*. "I don't know why Vaughn didn't bring Ruby with him tonight. I was so caught up in my own role in the evening, I didn't think to ask him."

Hoping to redirect her companion, Abigail pointed to a rabbit tucked into a nook between tree roots.

"I think the bunny would be a fun carving to bid on. All the younger kids will find him since he's low to the ground like them." Abigail glanced in Vaughn's direction, ready for rescue before his mother's questions became more personal.

He'd been heading their way at one point, but he'd been intercepted by an older man, who held him in deep conversation now.

The party around the tree had grown, with some additional guests from upstairs joining them as the original group still searched the branches for surprise forest critters to bid on in the fund-raiser.

"Perfect." Mrs. Chambers passed over her card to Abigail. "Would you mind penciling in the necessary details, my dear? I left my reading glasses at home tonight." She grinned ruefully as she held up a beaded evening bag. "I ask you, how could I fit more than a lipstick in this?"

"Of course." Abigail wrote the name of the carving on the card.

"And I don't mean to put you on the spot, Abigail, but I'm so very glad to see you with my son. Together."

Abigail looked up slowly, unsure how to respond. "We're not really together."

His mother attempted to smile but there were worried lines etched around her eyes. "But there was something in his manner when he called you over. He likes you, Abigail. I can tell."

Abigail could see how much his mother wanted to believe that, but she couldn't afford to bear the weight of anyone else's hope. She could hardly corral her own runaway feelings when she knew that Vaughn wasn't ready for more. She'd almost made the mistake of inviting Vaughn to the ultrasound and gender-reveal appointment with her. It wouldn't be fair to his mother to let her think that Vaughn was interested in anything long-term with Abigail.

"We've struck up a friendship, Mrs. Chambers," she assured her as she returned the bid card, her heart in her throat. "But..." She blinked fast. Took a breath to steel herself. "That's all we will ever be."

Needing to leave before her emotions spilled over, she excused herself. Turning, she ran squarely into Vaughn.

He must have overheard her. Although why her words would make his expression turn so thunderous, she couldn't say. She'd simply told his mother the truth, which Vaughn had stressed from the beginning of their relationship.

It wasn't destined to go anywhere. The sooner she began to realize that, the better.

Vaughn wasn't sure what had transpired between Abigail and his mother before she denied having a relationship with him. But the hurt in Abigail's eyes spoke for itself. She was upset.

She edged past him now, taking fast strides toward the exit. Thankfully, Vaughn's father had joined them, so he didn't have to leave his mother standing all alone in the middle of the gala fund-raiser.

"I need to speak to her," he informed his parents, leaning in to give his mother's cheek a kiss. "Thank you both for coming."

He charged through the crowd and headed up the stairs to the rooftop party, where the country band had taken the stage under the canopy of white lights. Steel guitars and fiddles had the dance floor almost full as the party turned lively.

His gaze scanned the tables, searching. Finally, he spotted a flash of scarlet-colored tulle near the sparkling water station by the bar. Abigail had a wrap over one arm and her evening clutch in her hand as she paused to take a drink.

Relief filled him. She hadn't left.

"Abigail." He reached her side, realizing as he approached that she was more upset than he realized. Her eyes looked shiny. Too bright.

He didn't think it was a coincidence that she chose that moment to set aside her glass.

"I was just leaving." She slipped the sheer black wrap she carried around her shoulders, tying it in front. "I'm more tired than I realized. I think the long days of working on the statue are catching up with me."

He heard the exhaustion in her voice. And while he had no doubt this week had been hard for her, he couldn't help but wonder if the conversation with his mother had more than a little to do with her sudden departure.

"I'd like to drive you home." He needed to speak to her. Wanted to keep her safe.

"Thank you. But I'll be fine." She opened her bag and pulled out her keys while the country band shifted the music for a slow number.

"Abby, please." He put a protective arm around her as a new rush of people lined up at the bar nearby. He drew her farther from the noise of the party, toward the display of flowers at one end of the rooftop garden. "I'm sorry if my mother made you feel uncomfortable in any way. She means well."

"Of course she does." Abigail shook her head.

"Your parents were both lovely. I just—" She hesitated. "I'm ready to leave."

"And I don't like the idea of you going home alone at night with Rich Lowell still at large."

"You were kind enough to install an alarm system to keep me safe," she reminded him, sliding her key ring over her finger while the metal jangled softly.

"But I'll sleep better if I see you walk inside." He couldn't seem to remove his hand from the small of her back, and wished he had the right to hold her in front of the world. To kiss her here and now. "The conversation with Cole Sullivan put into perspective just how dangerous Rich might be."

She chewed her lip. "I will be careful. But I have to consider another danger, Vaughn, and weigh it against the threat Rich poses." Her voice lowered as she spoke.

"I don't follow." He tipped his head closer to hear her. "What other danger could you possibly be worried about?"

"The emotional kind." Her dark brown eyes locked on his for a long moment. "The danger of falling for you has become very real for me. I can't take that lightly, and I can't allow myself to forget that only a foolish woman would lose her heart to someone who has no intention of ever returning it."

His gut sank. Or maybe it was his heart. He didn't know. Couldn't navigate his own emotions on the best of the days, and this was turning out to be far from his best day. His hand fell away from where he'd been touching her. He tipped his head back to glance up through the canopy of lights to see the night sky. Winking stars.

"Is that why you told my mother that we'll never be more than just friends?" The last snippet of conversation he'd heard returned to chastise him.

Sucker punch him.

"It's what you've been telling me from the very beginning." She toyed with her keys, flipping one back and forth on the ring, a nervous movement. "I simply tried to be honest with your mom before she got excited seeing us as a couple."

He deserved that kind of kick to the stomach. He'd set himself up for it, making sure Abigail knew he couldn't play a bigger role in her life, but wanting more anyway.

"I would still call us more than friends." When he thought about everything he'd shared with this incredible woman, he knew she was much more to him than a mere word like *friend* could ever express.

Her hand fisted around her keys, her jaw tensing. "Which is why you introduced me as *the artist* to your parents." She straightened, taking a step back. "At least I labeled us *friends* as opposed to implying we were merely professionals who briefly worked in the same building."

"That's not fair." His pulse quickened, and he sensed her pulling away. He wasn't ready for that.

Especially when he needed to keep her safe while Rich was still on the loose. "I purposely tried to keep the introductions light so I didn't put you on the spot. We hadn't talked about how to deal with situations like that. I didn't want to make assumptions about what you would prefer, so I erred on the side of being less personal."

She closed her eyes for a moment. When she opened them, she met his gaze head-on, her expression serious.

"So you were protecting me." She nodded. "I can accept that, and thank you for it even. But it doesn't change the fact that my life is about to get very complicated. I can't afford to have feelings for someone who isn't ready to be a part of that."

A shout went up from the dance floor as the band announced a popular line dance starting. Even in tuxedos and evening gowns, a group of partygoers responded to the call.

"A baby is not a complication." His gaze dropped to the small swell of her pregnancy. He recalled the thought that crossed his mind when he'd introduced her to his parents. That he wished he could claim both Abigail and her child as his own. "You're going to be an incredible mother."

Her smile was shaky. Sad. "That doesn't change the fact that you don't want to be a part of this."

"How can I be when I can barely sleep through the night on my own? I'm a grown man limping through life with the help of a dog. Working tire-lessly because I feel my professional skills are all I have to offer anyone."

Frowning, Abigail reached out to lay a hand on his chest. "That's not true."

"Every word of it is accurate." He wouldn't lie to her and he refused to lie to himself. "And it's not that I don't want to be a part of your life, Abigail. I just won't be the dark cloud hanging over you when you're ready for a vibrant, happy future."

He thought about her artwork and the way people loved it because of her perspective. Part of that per-spective was optimism. Joy. Her world was a place where fairies and forest creatures hid in the trees, waiting to be found. His world was a place that made him afraid to fall asleep.

"I can't make you take a gamble on us if you're not ready to." Straightening, she let her hand fall away from where she'd touched him. "I had hoped you might attend the baby's ultrasound appointment next week and be there when I find out the gender." She caught her lip between her teeth. "But I under-stand you're struggling with other things. And I don't want to cause you more stress."

"That's…" He couldn't even express how much that meant to him. That she'd wanted him there.

Too bad he'd already told her how much of a defi-cit he would be in her life.

"It's all right." She backed up a step. "You don't have to explain. I'm going to head out now."

He read between the lines.

Heard her saying goodbye to him loud and clear.

"I'm sorry, Abigail."

"So am I, Vaughn. More than you know."

Twelve

We want to be there with you.

On the morning of her ultrasound appointment, Abigail sat in the exam room in her cotton gown and reread the text Vaughn had sent her after the hospital summer gala. The text had a photo attached of him and Ruby. When she'd left the party that night—left him—her heart had felt like it was cracking in a thousand pieces. Spider cracks in every direction, like tempered glass before it falls apart.

And then his message had arrived, asking to be a part of this very big next step in her pregnancy. In her future.

The words made her smile now as she pulled the

note up on her phone. She clicked on the photo of him and Ruby to enlarge it, a man-and-dog selfie of the two of them sitting in the spare bedroom, where she'd slept the night she went to Vaughn's house. The photo touched her in a million ways. Made her think she was missed. Gave her hope that Vaughn was ready to tackle his PTSD even more aggressively since he'd been reluctant to bring Ruby into his workplace before now.

Because her ultrasound was in the medical arts wing of Royal Memorial, close to Vaughn's office, surely his colleagues would see him with Ruby today, even though he'd traded shifts with another surgeon in order to be here. He'd texted her he was on his way a few moments earlier. As she waited in the exam room, she wondered who would walk through the door first. The ultrasound technician, or Vaughn and Ruby.

When a quick knock sounded, she set aside her phone.

"Come in." She'd been left alone to change, but the technician—Leslie—had given her more than enough time to slip off her dress and put on the hospital gown.

"All set?" Leslie asked, stepping into the room.

"I'm ready." Abigail's heart sank for a moment, however, her eyes greedy for a sight of Vaughn.

"That's good, because you have a hospital celebrity joining us today." Leslie held the door open wide, admitting the sexy doctor Abigail had been hoping to see.

Ruby's nails clicked softly on the floor as she entered the room with Vaughn, who was dressed in street clothes. Dark pants and a fitted blue polo shirt. Abigail's breath caught just seeing him. He had an undeniable physical effect on her. She couldn't have pulled her gaze away from him if she tried.

"Thank you for letting us be here," Vaughn said quietly as her bent to kiss her cheek, his fingers lingering on her face for an extra few moments.

"It's good to see you. Both." Her skin tingled pleasantly where he touched her, a shiver tripping down her spine.

"We missed you." His eyes held hers while the technician logged in to her machine.

"I'm ready when you are, Miss Abigail," Leslie called to her. "Doctor Chambers, bring whatever chair is more comfortable for you."

Excited and oddly nervous, Abigail laid down on the table, then Leslie quickly covered her legs with one blanket and gave her a second if she wanted it for her breasts. After sliding her gown open, the technician squeezed the gel on Abigail's stomach to help her slide the wand for a good picture.

Vaughn leaned over to grasp her hand, his expression serious. Was he nervous, too? She thought her anxiety came from not knowing what her future held with a man she was falling for. Did his presence here mean he wanted to have a role in her life and the life of her child? But she wasn't sure why Vaughn appeared so…stoic. Quiet.

Perhaps bringing the dog into the hospital had already opened him up to comments and questions from Royal Memorial staffers before he even set foot in the exam room. But she was just guessing, unsure of so many things when it came to Vaughn.

The ultrasound screen lit up with images of the tiny life inside her, drawing her attention away from the worries to focus on the joys.

"Here we go," Leslie said cheerily, using the wand to hover over different parts of Abigail's belly as she pointed out parts of the baby. "Smile and wave for the camera, little one."

"Can you tell the sex?" Abigail asked, marveling over the images on the display monitor that would give her a video file afterward. "I'm hoping we'll know this time."

"I like to be really sure before I say anything." Leslie smiled, moving over and over one small spot on Abigail's stomach. "But by now, I feel certain." She glanced over at Abigail. "It's a girl."

A little girl. The words made happy tears fill Abigail's eyes. A lump formed in her throat as she looked toward Vaughn, wanting to share the moment.

He stared at the monitor, eyes narrowed. Worry etched between his eyebrows. Ruby leaned heavily against his side, far more in tune with her handler's moods than Abigail had been.

"Vaughn?" she said uncertainly. "I'm so excited."

His face cleared, but it seemed as though it took some effort on his part. He rubbed her arm. "Me, too." He swallowed. Scavenged a ghost of a smile. "That's incredible news."

Something was bothering him, though. And it upset Abigail that she didn't know what, but she tried to let it go and just enjoy the moment. She closed her eyes, listening to the sound of her heart beating over the monitor and the click of the technician's fingers on the keyboard as she zoomed in on various parts of Abigail's baby. The antiseptic scent of the paper-covered exam table distracted her, and she opened her eyes with a start, her senses sharpening rather than relaxing. She couldn't shake the sensation that Vaughn wasn't fully present with her on this important day.

"What's wrong?" she asked, needing him to be supportive or…to not be here at all. She'd really thought they'd moved past this and he was looking forward to being a part of today with her.

He didn't answer. He moved around the bed and approached the display monitor, as if to take a closer view. To Leslie, he asked, "Can you go back here for a second?" He gestured to a point to the left of the center.

Worry stirred inside her.

Real worry.

Ruby must have felt it, too, because the dog lifted her head away from Vaughn's thigh long enough to nuzzle Abigail's calf for a moment. A nuzzle of comfort.

Was this the way Vaughn felt when the golden retriever pressed herself to him? She couldn't imagine feeling this kind of anxiety all the time. Through her own fears, she couldn't deny a pang of renewed empathy for Vaughn.

The ultrasound technician circled the same spot over and over as both of the medical professionals in the room leaned closer to the screen, freaking Abigail out.

"Excuse me for just one second, okay?" Leslie stood, already moving toward the door. "I'm going to have our radiologist join us so she can give you the official reading."

Leslie patted Abigail's calf on her way past the bed, too. An absent gesture, imparting more comfort. Something wasn't right with her baby. She could feel it.

"Vaughn, is my baby okay?" Fear clogged her throat. She stared at the screen, willing her eyes to find whatever it was that they were seeing.

"This is a long way from my field of expertise." He shook his head, deflecting what should have been an easy question. "The radiologist will tell us more."

Vaughn looked pale. Distressed. His eyebrows knit.

"More about what?" Levering up on her elbows, she felt truly scared.

She had already lost her sister. She couldn't possibly lose her baby girl, too.

Vaughn's green eyes turned to meet hers. Serious. Unwavering. "I don't know. But if anything is wrong, you will have the best care in the world. I promise."

He gripped her hand in his, his assurance helping her to catch her breath even as it reinforced her fears. What was wrong?

When the radiologist stepped into the room, tucking a pen into the pocket of her lab coat, the specialist's eyes went briefly to Ruby in her service vest before glancing up at Vaughn and Abigail.

"Dr. Chambers." The woman—Dr. Oma, according to her badge—nodded at him as she took a seat in front of the ultrasound display and rolled the chair up to the work station. "Miss Stewart, I'm going to take a few more photos," she announced, moving the wand over Abigail's belly again. "I ran into your OB in the hall since he delivered a baby this morning, and I was able to consult with him briefly."

"Is he coming in?" Abigail wanted someone, anyone, to give her answers about what was happening.

Vaughn remained by the head of the bed with Ruby, his hand on Abigail's shoulder as he studied the screen behind the radiologist.

"Dr. Prevardi asked me to have Doctor Troy Hutchinson join us instead. If he has time." The ultrasound wand moved back and forth, pressing. The machine paused frequently for screen captures, zooming in on parts of Abigail's baby she couldn't possibly identify without someone explaining what she was seeing.

Beside Abigail, she heard Vaughn's sharp intake of breath.

"Who is he?" Abigail's eyes went from Vaughn to the radiologist.

"Dr. Hutchinson specializes in maternal-fetal medicine." Dr. Oma turned the display monitor toward Vaughn and Abigail. "We want to get his take on this." She circled a spot with her finger—dark blobs on the screen as far as Abigail could tell. "It's a small abnormality in the kidneys and we want to either rule out a problem or address it if there is one."

The radiologist continued to speak. Abigail knew because the woman's mouth moved, but the blood rushed in her ears so loudly that it drowned out everything else. Her brain couldn't process the news.

There was an abnormality in her baby. Her beautiful little girl might have something wrong with her.

Abigail felt like she was being sucked down a tunnel, a dark swirl of fears that blocked out everything else. By the time the specialist, Dr. Hutchinson, strode into the room, she was a mess.

She'd never been so grateful for Vaughn's presence, since he spoke the same language as the rest of the room, giving her the option of closing her eyes for some of the discussion about monitoring the defect. She swiped at the tears leaking down the side of her cheeks. Tears that Ruby must have noticed because she laid her doggy head right by Abigail's shoulder, her dark brown eyes filled with concern.

Later, when Abigail had calmed down some, she would ask Vaughn for his perspective on everything that happened today. He would give her an idea of how worried she ought to be. For now, she held his hand tight while Dr. Hutchinson promised to run more tests and get back to her soon.

Fixing Abigail something to eat back at her house that afternoon, Vaughn acknowledged he had overestimated himself. Overestimated how much he could change in order to be with Abigail.

Still reeling from the ultrasound appointment, he knew he hadn't been the steadying presence she deserved. Knew he'd failed her when she needed him to be strong. But the news that something might be wrong with her baby had wrecked all his defenses. He wasn't ready to be the man she needed and deserved in her life.

He recognized it as soon as he'd seen the tiny shadow on the ultrasound screen. His failure ate away at him now as he peeled a cucumber to add to the salad he was making for her. Ruby stalked back and forth between the living room, where Abigail rested on the couch, and the kitchen, where Vaughn prepared a light meal.

This morning he had felt a connection to the life inside of Abigail. And he had wanted to be there for her today. That text he'd sent her after the gala came after a lot of soul-searching. He didn't want to be without her. But already, he could see how short of the mark he was falling as a partner. In the exam room, he'd been more than rattled—he'd been afraid he would shut down on her completely, retreat from her emotionally at a time when she needed more support than ever.

If Ruby hadn't been there, keeping him focused and engaged, he might not have gotten through the strained meeting with Hutch. The news that Abigail's baby might have a serious health defect terrified him.

Drying his hand on a dish towel, he tossed the vegetable peels in the trash and set the salad on a tray with flatware and a drink for her. He wanted her to rest and had insisted on driving her home, knowing she was in no shape to drive herself after that scare.

She was rightfully upset.

Vaughn would have Micah bring her car home from the hospital for her. Make sure she had everything she needed. Hell, he'd do anything she wanted to be sure she was safe and cared for during her pregnancy. Especially since Rich Lowell was still out there.

But Vaughn could no longer fool himself that he was doing her or her child any good by sticking around. The darkness inside him wasn't going away.

It would hound him for the rest of his life.

He'd felt it roar to the surface as soon as he'd seen the abnormality on the ultrasound display, his fears so strong he'd been afraid to share his concerns with Abigail, knowing he might overstate the need for further testing. Hutch had handled the news well, remaining positive at all times before making a date to see Abigail again.

That was a good thing. Vaughn was ready to admit her and monitor her 24/7. Not because the baby's issue was so severe. But because he couldn't fathom anything ever happening to Abigail or her child.

He would not be the man who dimmed Abigail's vibrant spirit with his anxiety.

As he entered the living room, Ruby glanced up at him, her tongue lolling out one side of her mouth before she lay down beside Abigail. The dog's vest was off for the day. She'd already worked hard.

Now, however, another stressful moment was upon them.

Steeling himself for the discussion that had to happen, Vaughn settled the tray of food on the coffee table. He hoped Abigail understood how much this was going to rip out his heart.

Ruby lifted her head again, sensing the tension. She got to her feet and padded over to him, sitting beside him.

"Abigail." Vaughn wished he was better with words. Wished he had some way to make this hurt less for both of them. Already his chest ached like a weight sat there, crushing his ribs.

"Aren't you going to join me?" Her gaze went to the single tray. The single plate of salad.

Time to make sure she understood.

"I can't." It was that simple. And that complicated.

"I know I asked to be there with you today." He stepped closer to her, dropping into the seat by the sofa. "I wanted to be a part of this next phase of your life."

Her dark hair spilled over the wide straps of a sundress she wore, red with white polka dots.

"I couldn't have gotten through that appointment without you." She reached for his hand and threaded her fingers through his.

Regret carved a deep hole in him.

He couldn't imagine going through the rest of his life without touching her again. Without feeling this connection.

But he untwined his fingers and stepped away.

"I can't do it, Abigail. I'm only going to end up hurting you and this sweet little girl that's arriving this fall."

Her jaw dropped as she stared up at him. Then she snapped it shut. Her eyes sparked. "I don't understand."

"You mean too much to me for me to check out on you when you need me most." He shouldn't have let the relationship go this far. He'd been weak when he'd sent her that text saying he wanted to be at the ultrasound appointment. "It's better for you if we end things now."

Hurt and anger wrestled inside her, battling for dominance.

They elbowed her insides harder than any unborn child ever could.

Setting her feet on the floor, she rose to stand in

front of him, not even trying to rein in the feelings after the scare she'd had today.

"You're walking away now? After you told me how much you wanted to be by my side today?" She'd been prepared to walk away after the gala on Saturday.

Yes, it had torn her apart to let things end. But she'd been ready to respect his wishes. She really thought he'd come to terms with the demons he battled so far. *He'd* been the one to insist on more, after all, knowing how hard it had been for her to let him into her life. And now, he was backing away. It hurt. So damn much.

"I thought—I hoped—I could be a part of your future." The anguish in his eyes was real enough. Ruby walked around him once, then leaned into him hard, pressing her head to his hip. "But I saw today how fast this facade I try to hold together could fall apart." He snapped his fingers. "Like that, Abigail." He shook his head. "That's not the kind of support system you deserve."

"That news would devastate anyone with a pulse!" She didn't want to raise her voice, but she felt it notching higher. "And you still have one, Vaughn, unless you've forgotten. Your life is a gift— something you should see better than most people after the service you gave your country. But you're frittering it away like it means nothing to you."

He looked stunned silent.

Said nothing.

And she realized she wasn't close to done.

"Don't you owe it to the brothers in arms you lost not to take your life for granted?" She blinked hard against a surge of grief for her sister, the wave so strong it threatened to level her. "My sister died, and I hate that. But if she had pulled through, Vaughn, she wouldn't squander her days, scared to live."

Vaughn's shoulders were tense. His features frozen. Expressionless. She'd lost him already, she could tell. And her angry words were only making him retreat further.

Ruby shifted her weight on her front paws. A tiny hint of her own anxiety. Abigail felt like the worst kind of heel, but if she didn't call out Vaughn for taking his happiness for granted, who would?

"I've given my life to my work," he said finally. "I'm making a difference the best way I can."

"A noble sacrifice." Who wouldn't admire the way he'd given up everything to be the best surgeon possible? The most giving? "But you're still breathing, Vaughn. I hope one day you take the time to enjoy it and find happiness."

He studied her with remote green eyes, the way he might study a case file or a difficult patient. Assessing.

"I'm sorry, Abigail." The simple words revealed the huge, yawning divide between them. "I wish it was that simple. But it's not. And I'm…so damn sorry."

She had no words to express how much that hurt her. How much *he* hurt her.

When she failed to speak, he gave a small nod. An acknowledgment that there was nothing more to say. "I'll show myself out."

He turned on his heel, Ruby following behind him.

Abigail covered her mouth with her hand to make sure she didn't call after him. Ruby, at least, spared her a glance back before they walked out of her house.

She felt something wet hit her collarbone and realized tears were sliding down her face. She swiped at them impatiently. No way would she spend tears on a man who hid behind his work at the expense of a real connection with anyone.

At the expense of love.

Closing her eyes, she didn't want to acknowledge that thought. She couldn't have possibly let herself fall in love with a man who would never risk his heart for her. And if she had, she wanted to go on denying it until her own heart stopped breaking.

Thirteen

The next morning, Abigail stared listlessly at her sketchbook.

Charcoal in hand, she hoped to draw something—anything—to take her mind off her worries for her baby. She hadn't slept all night, fear for her unborn child sending her to the internet to read everything possible about kidney defects detectable in utero. That, of course, only frightened her more.

And while it was wrong of Vaughn to join her for the ultrasound if he didn't plan on sticking around, she could recognize today that her reaction had been fueled by fears for her little girl. Emotions had been running high yesterday.

Now, she also had to contend with the hole in her

own heart over losing Vaughn. She gripped the charcoal tighter between her fingers and sighed. She'd been in her seat by the studio window for almost twenty minutes now, and she had nothing to offer the blank page. No inspiration. No emotion.

She wished she could at least express her anger. Her frustration. But her tears were spent now after a sleepless night. Even the anger had faded since she'd vented her emotions on Vaughn the day before. She still felt the same crushing disappointment about what he'd done, yet, she sure did regret the way she'd expressed those things to him. Setting down the charcoal, she shoved aside the sketchbook and stared out the window instead, her gaze tracking a hummingbird bobbing around the special red feeder she'd installed so she could watch them drink. Bright emerald and blue, the bird darted in to press its long beak into the sugar water.

Not even the sight of her favorite feathered friend inspired her.

She regretted accusing Vaughn of not living his life. And, knowing how hard he battled his PTSD, she regretted suggesting how he should honor his fallen comrades in arms. It hadn't been her place. She would have bristled if someone told her how she should or shouldn't be honoring Alannah's memory.

There was no right way to grieve.

Restless, she moved to her carving tools instead, taking a seat at a table where she did detail work to play with a thick piece of hickory that hadn't spoken to her yet. The grain was wavy and warped, the lines moving in unexpected directions—maybe a branch had fallen away, giving the tree a lumpy knot to heal over. She traced the misshapen bits with her finger before tugging on a pair of gloves and picking up a gouge.

There was interest in the misshapen. Unlike things that were traditionally beautiful—perfectly formed with symmetry that pleased the eye—there was a different kind of beauty in nature's scars. The odd line that made you look a second time. The unexpected angle that forced the eye to linger.

The healed-over scars were strong. The lumpy branch had gone on long after a part had fallen away. Tough but thriving.

Abigail gouged deeper and deeper. Around and around. She formed circles, not sure where they were going but liking the feel of the wood in her hands. The smoothness she brought to the wood without taking away the erratic look of the grain. She had moved onto the chisel, finding figures in the wood as she worked.

A baby in the middle of it all.

Just a tiny form, but a uniting presence in the center. And arms going around it. Fluid, slender arms. Then, around those, another pair. Strong and muscular.

The chime of her phone beside her dragged her

from intense concentration, making her realize that she'd found inspiration at last. Over an hour had vanished without her realizing it. For a moment, she nursed a foolish hope that it might be Vaughn.

But she didn't recognize the number on her caller ID, dashing the idea right away.

"Hello?" Straightening from her worktable, she juggled the phone to her ear and peeled off her gloves.

"Abigail?" a male voice asked. "This is Dr. Hutchinson."

She tensed, waiting to hear more news about her baby. "Thank you for calling," she said, managing to get the words out even though she felt like she'd been robbed of breath. Fear and hope made her neck prickle as she prayed the news was good. "Did you learn anything new?"

She'd been uncertain of his next steps when she left the hospital the day before, thinking she'd quiz Vaughn about it more when they got home. But after their argument, Abigail realized she'd never gotten to do that.

"Nothing definitive." His voice was even, the sounds of the hospital around him—monitors beeping, a phone ringing, the PA system making an announcement in the background. "But I spoke to a colleague who specializes in hydronephrosis—the condition I suspected your child might have."

She'd read about that, too, a dilation of the kidneys. The problem could range in seriousness and required monitoring after birth, but it wasn't life-threatening to her baby.

"Did you rule it out? Or do you think that's what it could be?" She drew in a breath. Held it.

"We haven't ruled it out." He sounded matter-of-fact, but not gravely serious. Was that a good sign? "But my colleague agreed with me that if there is hydronephrosis, it is only to a slight degree."

Swallowing the lump in her throat, she struggled to follow what he was saying. "That's good, right? How serious do you think it is?"

Gazing out her studio window, she hoped for good news with all her heart.

"We are always glad to know about things like this ahead of time," he explained as the background noise from the hospital behind him quieted. He must have stepped into an office or private hallway. "That's why we look carefully at the scan. But to answer your question, we are not concerned about your baby's development and don't need additional scans."

The air rushed out of her lungs so fast she had to hold on to the windowsill. Relief flooded through her.

"We will want to monitor the baby carefully at birth through the first few days to be sure the kidneys function properly so we can intervene quickly if necessary," Dr. Hutchinson continued, "but treatment would be a short or more prolonged course of antibiotics. Nothing surgical."

Abigail felt like a boulder of worry had just rolled off her shoulders. Her baby would be fine. Healthy.

"Thank you so much." She wanted to shout it from the rooftops that her baby girl was all right. "I'm so happy I don't know what to say."

On the other end of the call, the doctor surprised her with a warm chuckle. "As a new father to triplets, I assure you, I can identify with what you're feeling. Nothing is more important to a parent than the health of their children."

As she disconnected the call, feeling like she had a new lease on life, her first thought was to contact Vaughn. He would want to know the baby was healthy.

But would that be fair to him after the way she'd lashed out at him for drawing away? Her chest ached with the knowledge that it wouldn't be right to call him now. No matter what, she loved Vaughn. She couldn't deny that in the clear light of day now that she'd had more time to process the shock and hurt of the breakup. Yes, she still hurt from losing him. Yet she wanted him to be happy, even if that meant living the isolated life he'd chosen.

She pulled her gloves back on and slid her safety goggles into place, taking her seat at the workbench. She would lose herself in her art for a little while, needing to give a voice to the knot of emotions inside her.

At least she knew what she was sculpting now. A little statue that she would send as a gift to Vaughn. A small way to apologize for hurting him. It didn't begin to patch the hole in her heart. But maybe, with any luck, it would help bring him a measure of peace to know that she and her baby still cared about him.

And always would.

Vaughn smashed a tennis ball across the net on the courts behind the Texas Cattleman's Clubhouse, venting his frustration with his racket.

His opponent, Hutch, the same doctor who had read Abigail's ultrasound scans, shocked him by returning the ball with an athletic backhand from the line.

A return shot Vaughn couldn't possibly reach.

Damn.

That meant he'd lost the game and the set along with it.

"Nice shot," he admitted grudgingly, sweat dripping down his back in the unrelenting Texas sun.

They'd started playing early to get ahead of the heat, but they'd tied in game after game, extending the set far longer than Vaughn had imagined they would be playing. He had finally tracked down Hutch for a round of tennis, selfishly hoping to reassure himself about Abigail's ultrasound. Vaughn knew better than to violate her privacy, not that Hutch would have allowed it. But since Abigail had invited him to be in the room during the scan, he thought that at least allowed him to know if he should be worried—if he should stop by and see Abigail or lend his professional weight to finding the best specialist the country had to offer. He would call in every favor he had to make sure she had the care she needed— even if she didn't want him around.

"I surprised myself." Hutch grinned. "I think that burst of speed was fueled by the fear I was going to have to forfeit if we tied another game." Shaking his head, he stalked toward the bench on one side of the courts, where there was a canopy for shade. "I'm not going to be able to move tomorrow."

Vaughn joined him at the bench where they'd left their bags and Ruby, in full view of the court and inside the fenced area for her safety. He dug in his cooler for a fresh water bottle and cracked open the cap, topping off Ruby's dish before he released her to play, giving her one of his old tennis balls. The retriever could catch almost anything in midair.

"I seriously doubt that." Vaughn yanked off his headband and tossed it in the bag along with his racket. "Recover fast so I can have a rematch and restore my honor."

"Sure thing." Hutch found his own cold drink and dropped onto the bench. He took the ball Ruby had already returned and tossed it to her again, the dog happily chasing it after her quiet time in the shade during the tennis match. "Have you spoken to Abigail recently?"

Regret mixed with guilt. "No."

A situation he planned to remedy immediately.

"I think you should get in touch with her." Hutch's eyes met his.

Vaughn sank to the bench beside his friend, thoughts of Abigail—of how he failed her—a weight on his shoulders. On the tennis court next to them, a foursome set up for doubles. The club was quiet, even for a weekday, the immaculate grounds mostly empty. A couple of young mothers sat poolside with small children in floaties, a lifeguard helping them keep the youngsters safe.

That would be Abigail one day, playing with her baby girl. Vaughn wanted to be in that picture of the future with her. With her child.

"I will."

"She deserves your support." Hutch swung to face him, mopping a towel over his head while Ruby waited for another turn to retrieve the old tennis ball, her tail wagging slowly.

"I—" He didn't know how to admit how badly he'd screwed up. "I wanted to make things work with her. She's the most..." He couldn't even come up with the words to describe Abigail. She was so beautiful, inside and out. So warmhearted and generous. A bright light to everyone around her. "The most incredible woman I've ever met. But I panicked when I heard about the baby."

Shame and remorse filled him. She deserved a better man than him. That was the only facet of the breakup he didn't regret. She should be with someone who would be there for her no matter what.

"What do you mean?" Hutch pulled two oranges out of his cooler and passed one to Vaughn. "As in, you're not ready to be a dad?"

"No. That's not it." Taking the orange, he started to peel it, understanding in retrospect what had made him run. "I am already attached to that baby. But what kind of partner will I make for Abigail when I need to run home and hide out with Ruby every time life gets tough?" Breaking off a section of the orange, he shook his head, more certain than ever of his decision. "If Ruby hadn't been there during the ultrasound, I might have lost it."

He didn't understand how to deal with his emotions anymore. They came at him too fast, too hard, and they carried memories of times he didn't want to remember. And no matter how much therapy he underwent, he couldn't imagine his future being any different.

"But you didn't," Hutch reminded him. "And if there's anything in life worth breaking down over, it's your kids." The toughest competitor on any Royal Memorial sports team pounded his fist lightly against his chest. "I don't mind telling you I would lose it if someone said my kids were in danger. That's the worst life can dish out, man. And you dealt with it."

Hutch took pity on Ruby and threw her another ball. The dog ran like the wind and leaped to catch it.

Vaughn hung his head, wishing he were a different man. A better one. "I dealt with it by telling Abigail I wasn't ready for more. By walking away when she needed me most."

"It didn't come easy for Simone and me, either," Hutch admitted while the doubles match nearby got underway. "All I know is that if you regret breaking things off, you should tell her."

"How would she trust me after that?" Vaughn would not hurt her again. He couldn't do that to someone he loved. The thought stopped him up short.

Loved?

Hell yes, loved.

On some level he'd known it this week when he'd felt like his heart had been ripped out of his chest with missing her. But now, there was no more hiding from the truth. He loved Abigail.

Hutch said nothing. Waited.

"I wouldn't trust me," Vaughn answered the question for him. He couldn't ask that of her, either. "Not after how I walked out on her."

"Maybe not," Hutch agreed easily, packing up his bag and tossing his orange peel in the trash. "But you're not Abigail. She might see something in you—something better—that you can't."

Promising a rematch soon, his tennis partner strode away from the courts toward the clubhouse.

Leaving Ruby and Vaughn alone.

He needed to shower and head into work. He was taking another doctor's afternoon shift—the trade for having the day off when he'd gone to the ultrasound appointment.

Packing up his tennis bag, he noticed a clubhouse staff member headed his way, carrying a package.

"Dr. Chambers," the younger man called to him. "I'm one of the valets."

"Is there a problem with my car?" Vaughn asked. He couldn't afford to be late for work.

"No, sir." The liveried staffer thrust the package toward him. "Someone named Brandon dropped this off for you. He said he thought it might be important."

Vaughn took the brown-wrapped paper box and noted the return address that had come by special shipment. Abigail Stewart.

Curious and trying not to feel too hopeful, he handed the valet a few bills and started tearing open the paper.

"Um. Sir?" The valet hadn't gone away.

Vaughn kept tearing the paper, finding a box inside. "Was there anything else?"

"You gave me all twenties." The valet looked perplexed as he stared at the tip.

With good reason. Vaughn hadn't even noticed what he was giving him.

"Keep it." The package in his hand represented the only bright spot in the last week, and he wasn't the kind of man who took money out of the hands of someone who'd helped him. "This was important."

The guy—a local college student, he guessed—grinned from ear to ear. "Thank you, sir. I'll share it with my partner out front who covered for me."

Once he was alone, Vaughn turned back to the box, dropping onto the bench again to open it. Ruby stared at it with him, setting aside her tennis ball, as if she knew how important a package from Abigail might be.

His throat burned, emotions creeping up on him fast. What if she was simply returning some personal possession he'd left behind? Something that fell out of his pocket at her house?

But it felt too heavy to be something he would have ever left at her place. Shoving aside the tissue paper, he found a note penned in careful, artistic calligraphy.

We are here for you.

The words—so unexpected—made his eyes burn along with his throat. Only this time, the burn was good. Hopeful. Hope-filled.

Tearing through more tissue, he saw a wood carving inside. He lifted it out with both hands, holding whatever she'd made like the treasure it was.

The sculpture was of two sets of arms—one male, one female—encircling a baby. A family.

One Abigail somehow still seemed to want him to be a part of, despite everything.

Hutch had suggested Abigail might be a more forgiving, trusting person than Vaughn. That she might still be able to move forward with him even though he didn't feel whole. His friend was right.

Vaughn had a second chance at happiness. At the life Abigail warned him he was squandering.

He wouldn't waste this one.

Fourteen

Abigail reeled in her measuring tape as she stood against the east wall of the children's ward lounge. She tried to imagine what limbs she had at her studio that would work for the treehouse she had planned for phase two of the interactive art installation. The play space would be a raised platform just a few feet off the ground, but it would be surrounded by fabric leaves and a sculpture that looked like a giant nest, enhancing the sense of being high in the air.

The hospital hummed with activity nearby, now that the partition had been removed so patients could enjoy the tree sculpture. She would have to plan her future installation dates carefully, waiting to assemble the rest once she had significant portions prebuilt in her studio. Brandon had left her messages already, hoping to help.

His kind offer had seemed so genuinely motivated by an interest in her work that she couldn't refuse. And she had fun sharing her craft with someone so obviously intrigued. Even if seeing him would remind her of Vaughn and all that she'd lost.

Blinking away the thought of him that she knew would only add to her heartache, Abigail tried to focus on the work she adored instead of the man she loved. She had promised herself that—for her baby's sake—she needed to find joy and happiness again. She'd told Vaughn to do that, so she felt like she needed to at least try to follow her own advice, even if it was easier said than done.

"There's a fairy!" a youthful voice shouted nearby, the thrill of discovery obvious in the raised, excited octave.

Abigail smiled, grateful for the distraction from her sad thoughts. Turning, she spotted a familiar redhead pointing high up in the tree.

Zoe. The patient she'd met when she'd been sculpting the *Tree of Gifts*. Only this time, the little girl was no longer in a hospital gown or attached to an IV. She held the hand of an auburn-haired older woman whose features were startlingly similar to her own. It could only be the child's mother.

Abigail retrieved her purse and walked toward the pair. A handful of other children and their families dotted the lounge. A few of the kids were in pajamas or hospital gowns, wearing hospital ID bracelets. Others seemed to be visiting siblings or friends. But it pleased Abigail to see that all of them were interacting with the tree in some way. Admiring it, touching it, searching for creatures or reading the placard the hospital had let her install after the gala.

For Alannah, the brightest bird of all.

It made Abigail happy to think of her sister that way—a part of nature. A continuing presence in Abigail's art. A joyous aspect of her own perspective.

Arriving near the little girl and her mother, Abigail smiled at the redheaded pixie who had wanted to know if she was really carving a tree from a tree.

"Hello, Zoe." Abigail tucked her measuring tape in her handbag before introducing herself to the girl's mother. "I'm Abigail. Zoe and I met when I was working on the tree."

"I found a fairy, Miss Abigail!" Zoe announced in a very loud, excited whisper, as if she didn't want to give it away for the other children. "Just like you said."

The girl's mother smiled warmly. "I'm Rita." She stuck out her hand and shook Abigail's. "Zoe told us all about your tree. She wouldn't rest until we came back to search for fairies since she was discharged before you were finished."

Touched, Abigail was very glad she'd made something special for Zoe. After the health scare with her own little girl, she had renewed empathy for the hardship of families with children who battle illnesses. "I enjoyed meeting her. And I've been meaning to ask one of the nurses if they had a way to get a small gift to her."

Zoe had been staring up into the tree, perhaps seeking more creatures. But at the word *gift* she edged closer.

"For me?" she asked, green eyes bright.

"Yes." Kneeling down to Zoe's height, Abigail withdrew a small carving wrapped in a purple bandanna. "You inspired me to add fairies to the tree. They are there because of you. So I thought you should have one of your own to keep."

Zoe's eyes went cartoon-wide as she peered up to her mother, as if seeking permission to take the gift. At Rita's nod, the girl carefully cradled the carving in her hands, peeling aside the bandanna. Her eyes met Abigail's over the sculpture, her gratitude and wonder the most moving tribute to Abigail's work that she could imagine.

For a thank-you, the girl flung her arms around Abigail's neck and squeezed her, still clutching her fairy tight.

"I love her," she said, still in a whisper, but this time more heartfelt and sweet. "I'm going to call her Abigail."

"I'd like that." She wondered if the last statue

she'd made—the one she'd sent to Vaughn—had been received with nearly as much enthusiasm.

With an effort, she pushed aside thoughts of him to say goodbye to Zoe and Rita.

Now that she had the measurements she needed for the play area nest, she could leave Royal Memorial, too. Her feet were only reluctant, she knew, because there was always a chance of seeing Vaughn here.

Forcing her way toward the stairs, she turned to see Vaughn leaning against her tree in the lounge. Watching her.

Startled, even though people were coming and going in the lounge all the time, Abigail's mouth went dry.

In the few days since she'd seen him, she'd forgotten how devastatingly handsome he was. Still clean-shaven, he wore scrubs, the same as the day they first met. Awareness pricked over her skin. Her breath catching.

"That was a beautiful thing to do." Levering his shoulder off the tree, he stalked toward her. "You made that little girl's day."

Abigail's tongue stuck to the roof of her mouth, no matter that she'd wanted to see him. Hoped to see him. Played in her mind a thousand times what his reaction might be to her gift.

She hadn't anticipated how much she'd pinned her hopes on this man even though he'd walked away from her. She told herself to wait and see what he said. To listen with an open heart.

To be a better person than she'd been the last time they spoke. If nothing else, she would have the chance to apologize.

"She made mine, too." Her voice sounded funny in her own ears.

Vaughn halted a few steps from her. Close enough that she could reach out and touch him. Her pulse quickened, the way it always seemed to when he was near her.

"As much as she liked the statue you made her, I am willing to bet I liked the one you made for me even more." His gaze was steady. Sincere. "Thank you for that, Abigail."

Pleased he enjoyed the gift, she couldn't deny that she'd hoped for...more than that. A part of her had envisioned it as a peace offering. A way to heal things between them. She glanced around the lounge, wishing they could speak someplace privately. Then again, maybe it was better this way. She couldn't fall apart with an audience nearby.

"I'm sorry for the way I—" She had to clear her throat. "I shouldn't have come down on you so hard that day. I was hurting, and I took it out on you."

Vaughn pointed toward the chairs in the far corner of the lounge. "Would you sit with me for a minute? If you have time?"

Nodding, she walked beside him on wobbly legs.

She sat in one of the high-backed leather seats while Vaughn took the one opposite her.

"Abby, every single thing you said to me that day was true." His hands fisted where they sat on his knees, as if fighting an impulse. "I have been going through the motions of an existence that hardly counts as living. Going to work. Fighting off bad dreams. Rinse and repeat."

"You can't help that." She had read more about PTSD since their split, educating herself specifically about the problems veterans suffered. She wished she'd taken time to research more thoroughly sooner in their relationship. "That's why I shouldn't have pushed—"

"You had every right to push. Because I told you I wanted to be there with you." He unclenched his hands now and reached for hers. Held them tightly in his. "And maybe that's what needed to happen for me, Abigail. I've worked hard to live a normal life. And Ruby's been great. But it's like I hit a plateau and that was all I expected from my future. More of the same."

She stared down at where he held her hands, trying to make sense of that urgent touch in relation to his words. "I don't understand."

"When you came along, you pulled me off the plateau, bringing me higher and closer to whole. And it was great. I thought life might open up for me. That I could do more. Be more." He gentled his hold on her, smoothing his thumbs over her knuckles. Soothing them. "But when I froze up in the exam room—I knew I needed to be there for you and I felt like a blank slate. I was scared for you and that tiny child you carry inside you, but I knew it didn't even show on my face. It's like this filter goes up between me and how I feel."

"I remember." She thought back to that day, seeing it in a different light. Remembering how remote he'd seemed. "It didn't seem like you."

She'd been hurt even then, before she heard about the abnormality.

"Exactly. I came face-to-face with my own failing and I know you deserve better." He sounded too certain.

"What if I don't want better?" She thought about how happy it made her to fall asleep in his arms, even if he wasn't ready to share a bed with her for the full night. How much she loved enjoying a meal with him under the stars. Or sharing her artwork and seeing his eyes light up, like he understood what she was trying to create. "Vaughn, what if I want you, just the way you are?"

"Abigail. You deserve better, and that's what I want you to have." His voice brooked no argument.

Her heart fell. She dragged in a raw breath, ready to fight for him. For them.

But he spoke first. "If you'll give me another

chance, I can promise you that I will never, ever walk away from you again."

She blinked at the unexpected words. Had he really said what she thought he just said?

"Another chance?" Her voice sounded just like Zoe's had minutes before, a whisper that said she hardly dared to believe what she'd heard.

Vaughn let go of one hand to cup her cheek in his palm.

"I know I don't deserve you, but I do love you, Abigail. So much. And if you'll have me, I will spend the rest of my days making you and that little girl happy." His thumb stoked along her cheek.

Her heart swelled with love for him. Happiness beckoned and she wouldn't ever turn that away. She trusted his sense of honor. His commitment to what he said. She had been hurt so deeply by Rich that she had been guarding her heart carefully, fearing being taken advantage of again. But Vaughn Chambers was nothing like Rich Lowell. The doctor who sacrificed his career to help injured soldiers overseas was a selfless, caring man, and the oath he'd taken as a physician was something he took deeply to heart.

Now, he'd made a vow to her. And she trusted it implicitly.

"When I sent you that note, Vaughn, I told you we were here for you." She tugged their joined hands to her growing baby bump and placed his palm there. "I meant it. I love you."

His hand spanned the curve of new life and the baby fluttered with her own acknowledgment. His eyes widened. A hint of wonder inside the man who thought he didn't show anything to the world. Her heart melted.

"I'm here for you, too, Abby." He drew her close, kissing her with the tender promise of forever. "Both of you."

Her head tipped forward, touching his. She'd never felt so cherished. So precious. So loved. For a moment, she forgot everything else but him. When his lips claimed hers the next time, she clung to him, answering his kiss with a passion that simmered just below the surface.

From the opposite side of the children's ward lounge, someone started to clap. Someone whistled.

Turning as one with Vaughn, Abigail saw Dr. Hutchinson at the nurses' station just beyond the tree sculpture. He seemed to be the ringleader, still whistling, as other nurses and staffers peeked out of patient rooms to see what the fuss was about. A couple of cheers went up. Even a few parents in the lounge joined in the applause.

Vaughn gave the group—his colleagues—a thumbs-up that seemed to quiet them. He turned back to Abigail and kissed her again.

"Everyone loves a happy ending."

"I guess so." She laughed, a sound of joy spilling over. She couldn't be happier. And then she remembered she had even more good news. "Dr. Hutchinson said the baby is going to be fine, you know."

The raw emotion in Vaughn's eyes told her how scared he'd been. How much he already cared for this baby.

"That's the best news I could have asked for." His shoulders relaxed, his smile huge, lighting up the room. "I was prepared to call in every specialist nationwide to help Hutch with your case." Vaughn turned serious again, his commitment to her baby as deep as the one he'd made to her.

He would love and protect them both.

"Thank you." She laid a hand on his chest, grateful to have him back in her life. For good. "That means so much to me."

Vaughn stroked her hair. "Hutch told me it was okay to be terrified for the sake of your child. Normal." He squeezed his eyes closed. "I don't know why it helped to hear it from him, but I needed that different perspective to make me see I wasn't just detaching because of the PTSD."

"I'm all about seeing things through different eyes." Abigail had a career in art that she loved because of it. "And I'm so happy you think of this baby that way. As your child."

He was signing on for much more than being her partner.

"I can't wait to have you both in my life every day. To grow a family and find happiness together."

"What are we waiting for, exactly?" she asked. "I'm ready to start now."

His smile warmed her to her toes. She wanted to see it each day, even for a little while.

"Well, first, I need for my shift to end." He stood, drawing her to her feet with him. "I'm hoping no one noticed I went AWOL to flirt with the hot artist working in the children's ward."

"I won't tell," she promised, thinking about all she wanted to share with this man.

All she still wanted to find out about him.

"But I could pick you up on my way home tonight. Maybe bring you to the ranch for the night? Or forever?"

The question brought tears to her eyes on a day that had already brought her so much hope and promise.

"I would like that." She couldn't wait to be alone with him. To celebrate in private.

"Then I'll pick you up at eight thirty." He kissed her forehead, swiping a finger along her cheek to catch a happy tear. "And start the rest of our lives together."

She brushed her lips to his, standing on her toes. "It's a date."

* * * * *

COMING NEXT MONTH FROM

HARLEQUIN *Desire*

Available May 1, 2018

#2587 AN HONORABLE SEDUCTION

The Westmoreland Legacy • by Brenda Jackson

Navy SEAL David "Flipper" Holloway has one mission: get close to gorgeous store owner Swan Jamison and find out all he can. But flirtation leads to seduction and he's about to get caught between duty and the woman he vows to claim as his...

#2588 REUNITED...WITH BABY

Texas Cattleman's Club: The Impostor • by Sara Orwig

Wealthy tech tycoon Luke has come home and he'll do whatever it takes to revive his family's ranch. Even hire the woman he left behind, veterinarian and single mother Scarlett. He can't say yes to forever, but will one more night be enough?

#2589 THE TWIN BIRTHRIGHT

Alaskan Oil Barons • by Catherine Mann

When reclusive inventor Royce Miller is reunited with his ex-fiancée and her twin babies in a snowstorm, he vows to protect them at all costs—even if the explosive chemistry that drove them apart is stronger than ever!

#2590 THE ILLEGITIMATE BILLIONAIRE

Billionaires and Babies • by Barbara Dunlop

Black sheep Deacon Holt, illegitimate son of a billionaire, must marry the gold-digging widow of his half brother if he wants his family's recognition. Actually desiring the beautiful single mother isn't part of the plan, especially when she has shocking relevations of her own...

#2591 WRONG BROTHER, RIGHT MAN

Switching Places • by Kat Cantrell

To inherit his fortune, flirtatious Valentino LeBlanc must swap roles with his too-serious brother. He'll prove he's just as good as, if not better than, his brother. At everything. But when he hires his brother's ex to advise him, things won't stay professional for long...

#2592 ONE NIGHT TO FOREVER

The Ballantyne Billionaires • by Joss Wood

When Lachlyn is outed as a long-lost Ballantyne heiress, wealthy security expert Reame vows to protect her. She's his best friend's sister, an innocent... Surely he can keep his hands to himself. But all it takes is one night to ignite a passion that could burn them both...

HDCNM0418

Get 2 Free Books,
Plus 2 Free Gifts—
just for trying the Reader Service!

SPECIAL EXCERPT FROM

HARLEQUIN

Desire

*When Lachlyn is outed as a long-lost Ballantyne heiress,
wealthy security expert Reame vows to protect her. She's
his best friend's sister, an innocent... Surely he can
keep his hands to himself. But all it takes is one night to
ignite a passion that could burn them both...*

*Read on for a sneak peek of
ONE NIGHT TO FOREVER by Joss Wood,
part of her **BALLANTYNE BILLIONAIRES** series!*

That damn buzz passed from him to her and ignited the
flames low in her belly.

"When I get back to the office, you will officially
become a client," Reame said in a husky voice. "But
you're not my client...yet."

His words made no sense, but she did notice that he
was looking at her like he wanted to kiss her.

Reame gripped her hips. She felt his heat and...
Wow...

God and heaven.

Teeth scraped and lips soothed, tongues swirled and
whirled, and heat, lazy heat, spread through her limbs
and slid into her veins. Reame was kissing her, and time
and space shifted.

It felt natural for her legs to wind around his waist, to
lock her arms around his neck and take what she'd been
fantasizing about. Kissing Reame was better than she'd
imagined—she was finally experiencing all those fuzzy
feels romance books described.

It felt perfect. It felt right.

Reame jerked his mouth off hers and their eyes connected, his intense, blazing with hot green fire.

She wanted him… She never wanted anybody. And never this much.

"Holy crap—"

Reame stiffened in her arms and Lachlyn looked over his shoulder to the now-open door to where her brother stood, half in and half out of the room. Lachlyn slid down Reame's hard body. She pushed her bangs off her forehead and released a deep breath, grateful that Reame shielded her from Linc.

Lachlyn touched her swollen lips and glanced down at her chest, where her hard nipples pushed against the fabric of her lacy bra and thin T-shirt. She couldn't possibly look more turned-on if she tried.

Lachlyn couldn't look at her brother, but he sounded thoroughly amused. "Want me to go away and come back in fifteen?"

Reame looked at her and, along with desire, she thought she saw regret in his eyes. He slowly shook his head. "No, we're done."

Lachlyn met his eyes and nodded her agreement.

Yes, they were done. They had to be.

Don't miss
ONE NIGHT TO FOREVER by Joss Wood,
*part of her **BALLANTYNE BILLIONAIRES** series!*

Available May 2018 wherever
Harlequin® Desire books and ebooks are sold.

www.Harlequin.com

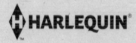